FOXY AND THE BADGERS

By the same author in Piccolo Books
FOXY

Also available in Pan Books
THE BEST CAT STORIES

FOXY AND THE BADGERS

JOHN MONTGOMERY

Illustrations by Prudence Seward

A Piccolo Book

PAN BOOKS LTD
LONDON

First published 1968 by George Allen and Unwin Ltd.
This edition published 1971 by Pan Books Ltd,
33 Tothill Street, London, S.W.1.

ISBN 0 330 02826 x

Printed in Great Britain by
Cox & Wyman Ltd,
London, Reading and Fakenham

TO JEREMY MORTIMER

FOXY AND THE BADGERS

Chapter One

I sometimes think, when I see him running around the lawn at the back of the farmhouse, or standing on a fallen tree trunk to sniff at the young leaves, or scampering eagerly along the hedgerows in search of rabbits, that I am the luckiest boy in the county of Sussex, if not in the whole world, to own such a companion.

You can't imagine anything more beautiful than my fox. The marking on his throat is pure white, his eyes are a glistening amber, his coat is silky red, and when he sits down his long rich brush twists warmly around his feet.

Perhaps it is his neat little teeth that make him so attractive. When he shows them – small, sharp and even – he seems to be smiling, almost enjoying a joke. He likes to share everything, the sunny days and the wet ones, and we are seldom apart. I'd say he is the best friend I could have chosen to live with on the farm at Woodmere.

When I first found him in the Great Wood on our pine-tree hill above the house, he was only a helpless cub. I brought him up secretly in the barn, unknown to my foster parents, Mr and Mrs Hedger, who had adopted me from the orphanage. Then, when they discovered him, they let him stay on condition that I cared for him myself, and kept him under control. That wasn't difficult. One thing Foxy and I have in common is that we are both orphans. So really, we look after one another. I'd be lost without him, and he's been brought up tame, to rely on me.

He was quite expensive at first, but my mate Charlie Elliott, whose father is our village butcher, used to smuggle pieces of meat out of the shop. Sometimes it was beef or mutton, often it was liver or veal, but Foxy likes rabbit best, and always knows when Charlie is near. I think he smells of the old butcher's shop, but of course he doesn't know it. That's a funny thing about foxes, they have the cleverest noses.

Old greedyguts, Charlie calls Foxy. But as the cub grew stronger and his coat turned from furry grey to smooth red, he became used to eating his meals with us in the parlour. Mum – that's what I call Mrs Hedger now – spoils him with milk and pieces of pie and sometimes even cream.

Foxy is the best watchdog you could find anywhere, no stranger is allowed to reach the front door without a bark or a growl to tell us that the fox has heard or scented the visitor. These days, Mr Outen the postman leaves the letters on the flint wall near the gate, because he once got nipped on the leg when Foxy crept up behind him.

I suppose the most terrible moment of my life, even

worse than the day I left the convent to start out on my own, was the time when the hunting people came to the farm and Foxy was out in the woods. I've never been sure how he managed to escape; I prayed for him, and somehow he came back. And I made certain, afterwards, that he never went off alone. Too many people don't understand that if you have a tame fox, brought up on the milk bottle, he's just like a dog, but more attractive.

What fun it is to take him out across the fields to the slate quarry, where the green grass snakes slide away under the stones at the sound of your step, and the blackbirds come hopping down on to the lower branches and turn their heads sideways to watch you pass.

He runs with his pink tongue hanging out on one side of his mouth, and he takes long powerful strides, moving quite silently. If you were a rabbit sitting close to a hedge you might hear him coming, but not if you were a human. His little feet go *pad*, *pad*, *pad*, quickly and silently. Not that he's ever caught a rabbit, and I wouldn't want him to. They're much too fast for him.

'Come on, Foxy!' I shout. 'You'll never make it!'

Once he disturbed a wasp's nest down by the watermill, and I had a terrible time trying to persuade him to come away. Foxes can be very obstinate.

'Foxy!' I called. 'Leave them alone! They'll sting you!' And of course, I was right. I took him home on

If you were a rabbit

the lead with a nasty swollen lip, his brush drooping low, and Mum bathed and painted the place with iodine and then sent him to bed. It was a very sorrowful cub that slept by my feet that night, curled up like a ball by the fire. He didn't know how it had happened. That's where he usually sleeps, on a special blanket at the end of the bed. He has to have his own blanket because sometimes leaves and pieces of bracken and earth cling to his pads. He's just like a dog, really.

We've got lots of friends down in the village. Miss Thring, our schoolteacher, let him enter for the dog race in the sports. They line all the dogs up on one side of the playing field with their owners at the other end and when the whistle blows we shout for our dogs to come to heel. Foxy beat them all by several yards, I was very proud of him. He ran just like a streak of lightning, and jumped up into my arms. They gave him a prize, a new collar and lead.

Our special friends, apart from Charlie, are Sue and Jimmy Norwell and Jeremy. Sue has spaniels at home, and she was the first person to give Foxy a collar of his own. She's about twelve, I think, and Jeremy is eleven. But not everyone in the village is so friendly as my schoolmates. Old Mr Tidy, who keeps the ditches clear of leaves and trims the roadside hedges up our way, looks on Foxy as a wild animal who has never been properly tamed. He's plain stupid, that old man, he thinks his chickens are all going to be eaten up overnight. I reckon he's so keen on eating his chickens himself that he doesn't want anyone else to get there first. It doesn't occur to him that Foxy is tame and has been taught never to look at fowls, and certainly never to chase them. Why, we've got two hundred chickens on our farm, and Foxy walks among them and they never even cluck, but just keep pecking away at the ground, as if he wasn't there.

'You watch out,' old Mr Tidy says. 'That Reynard of yours will get you into trouble one day, you mark my words. Don't say I didn't tell you.'

Silly old Mr Tidy. He doesn't know that if you feed animals properly and regularly and care for them, they don't need to go hunting for food.

Mr Tidy is stupid, but the person we really fear – or used to, I should say – is Mr Whiteway, who lives in a big house with iron gates down by the village green. Most of the land and woods belong to him and he keeps chopping down trees and selling them. Soon there won't be any woods left, he never plants any saplings. That's bad enough, but what is worse is that he shoots everything on sight. There isn't a pheasant or a rabbit or hare in the district which is safe when Mr Whiteway walks out with his double-barrel shotgun under his arm. He makes his money in London during the week and spends every weekend in Woodmere, banging away at wild animals and birds.

His wife is no better. Mr Tidy told me she could hit

a fast-moving hare at two hundred yards, and often did. I can't see why people live in the country if they want to make it like the towns, with no trees and animals. She wears tweedy clothes and sometimes she goes around in funny-looking trousers which make her look fat. I don't like the Whiteways at all. Their house is large and expensive and they have a swimming pool at the back, and two cars in the garage, a big low white Jaguar which dashes up the lanes frightening the dogs and cats, and a fast yellow station-wagon into which they throw all the creatures they slaughter. What they do with so many dead animals I can't imagine, but Jeremy told me old Whiteway has a room at the back of his house full of stuffed birds, like a museum; rooks, crows, pheasants, partridges, even little finches, and a robin. Fancy anyone shooting a robin. I reckon they don't like anyone to live except themselves.

At weekends the banging of the guns up in the woods sounds like a battle in the Wars of the Roses. The rabbits and squirrels and blackbirds would be well advised to leave the district on Friday night and not return until Monday morning, it would be much safer. Those Whiteways are just trigger-happy.

'Sounds like D-Day to me,' said Mr Tidy one Sunday morning, when I was bringing Foxy back on the lead from church. 'You'd better keep that creature of yours locked up, or they'll 'ave him for dinner. Shoot anything on legs, they will.' Mr Tidy smokes a very dirty old pipe, which smells. I kept up-wind of it.

'We stay right away,' I said. But I had often feared that sooner or later the Whiteways or one of their party would meet Foxy out for a walk, not realizing he was tame. That might be disastrous. So I always keep him on the lead whenever I hear the gunfire, or see the yellow station-wagon speeding along the lane.

One night Mr Whiteway took a farm jeep up into the woods and turned the headlights into the trees to hypnotize the rabbits. Then he started shooting. He was banging away up there for hours, almost until daybreak. The noise kept me awake, and Foxy lay with his head on my feet and twitched and whimpered and growled. He knew something was wrong, he's pretty bright about that kind of thing. Foxes are very sensitive.

I asked Dad next morning at breakfast if Mr Whiteway was allowed to kill all the animals without anyone stopping him.

'It's his land,' he said. 'As long as he doesn't shoot game out of season, or kill protected birds, he's doing nothing illegal. That's the law.'

'Then it's a rotten one,' I said. 'Besides, he kills magpies and thrushes and rooks and blackbirds and pigeons and – almost anything. Sometimes he doesn't stop to pick them up. I found a dead finch last week. It must have been him.'

Mum said, 'He's a very important person round

here. We don't want to have any difficulties with him.' That's the trouble with grown-ups, they're all afraid of one another, even sensible people like Mum and Dad. They don't want to upset the neighbours. Just because the Whiteways live in a big house and own two cars and have a blue swimming pool, I don't see why they have to kill everything in *our* wood. It's not reasonable, is it?

'Dad,' I asked. 'Do the woods really belong to Mr Whiteway? I always think of them as being ours.'

'He rents them with the buttercup meadow.'

'So he's allowed to shoot there?'

'Yes, he's the tenant. The Great Wood and Brock's Wood are both let to him.'

I just couldn't agree that people should be free to kill animals wholesale, any more than I'd accept Sue's casual remark that Foxy smelt funny. Everyone knows that a fox has a peculiar smell of its own, sometimes quite strong, and not always pleasant. It is this scent which attracts the hounds which are trained to follow and eventually to kill the fox.

'He doesn't half niff,' she said one day during the dinner break when we were all sitting under the trees on the edge of the green. I looked at Foxy, curled up near my feet, and felt annoyed.

'Not half as bad as your smelly spaniels,' I replied. You've got to be tough with girls, sometimes.

'Dogs are different,' she said.

'I don't see why. Foxy's as good as any dog, and

more brainy. Besides, he's more rare. Anyone can own a dog or a cat or a hamster, but how many tame foxes do you know?'

There wasn't any answer to that one. Sue just pulled a face and kept quiet. But that afternoon I was thinking how much I owed to Foxy, the first friend I made when I came to live in Woodmere. You simply hadn't time to feel bored or lonely or at a loss when there was a young fox tugging at the lead, rearing to take you for a walk, to go dashing into the buttercup meadow or up the hill to the Great Wood or along the mossy footpath to the stream. Every moment of his life is a vigorous adventure, and I share it with him. The only time he's quiet is when we return home, sometimes wet and muddy, always tired. Then he lies out full length on the cold stone slabs in the kitchen, with his heart pounding so loudly you can almost hear it.

We are nearly always together, and he was with me when I found the mysterious secret cottage in the middle of the Gipsy Wood; the house which was to play such an important part in our adventure that summer.

It was strange, the way we found it. I had explored the Gipsy Wood many times, but I had never been to the farthest end, where the brambles and tangles are thickest and the trees grow close together.

I remember the day well. It was a Saturday morning and Dad and Mum had gone into Horsham, shopping. I had planned to go down to Charlie's, to help him clean out his rabbit hutch, but he had a bad cold and was away from school on the Friday; which made me think the hutch wouldn't be cleaned out for another week, which would make it rather smelly. But Charlie, with a cold, wouldn't notice it.

I didn't know how to spend the afternoon. I had brushed and combed Foxy after breakfast, and I had taken a bucket of water into the pony's stable.

By ten o'clock I was kicking my heels at the end of the chicken run, without any plans. But if I didn't know what to do, Foxy did. That's the trouble with that dog, he must have his own way. He started by rolling about on the lawn, baring his teeth and making funny little barking noises. When we reached the chicken run he was already anxious to go, running up and down, swishing his brush, pawing at my legs. I knew exactly what he wanted.

'No,' I said. 'We're not going out. We're staying here. Just be quiet.'

It didn't make any difference. He rolled over and smiled again, and looked silly. As if he knew perfectly well that sooner or later I would have to take him with me.

'Oh, dry up,' I said. 'You'd walk the hind legs off an elephant. We're staying *here*.'

But of course we didn't. What can you do when you've got a fox that's crazy about walks, that is never happy unless he's lopping around the countryside with his nose to the ground and his ears twitching for rabbits? We went back to the house and I locked the back door and put the key under the secret stone, and took the leather lead down from the peg in the front porch. That did it, Foxy went berserk, you've never seen such a performance; anyone would think he'd never been taken out before. He leaped up so high towards my face that I thought he'd bite my nose.

'Come on, then,' I said. 'I'll race you to the stile.' So we were off, Foxy running far ahead, stopping now and again to turn and look back, just to make sure I was following. Sometimes I play a trick on him, hiding behind a tree when he isn't looking. He soon misses me, turns back, and starts to search. You have to keep dead still, but he always finds you in the end, though it's fun to see him sniffing away behind all the wrong trees until he catches your scent and comes leaping up at you. Sue plays the game with her spaniels.

When I reached the stile I was puffed, and started to walk. Foxy was far ahead, running along the edge of the stubble field, chasing the birds as they flew up in his path.

'Fox-e-e!' I called, and for a moment he paused and looked back at me, head up, a flash of pink tongue, his feet firm and strong. Then he turned and went on chasing the birds. You've grown into quite a strong fellow, I thought; it's all that meat and milk and exercise.

We went on down to the stream, crossed the mill bridge and climbed the meadow towards Gipsy Wood. I was quite hot with running, and I didn't see any object in hurrying any more, so I took my time. It was only when I reached the edge of the wood that I realized Foxy was missing. I couldn't hear him, there were only the usual bird sounds in the wood, chirping and twittering, and the noise of a train over by Horsham.

'Fox-e-e!' I called.

I may as well admit that I've never been attracted by the Gipsy Wood. People in the village say it's haunted, and no one goes there, it is much too overgrown. But Foxy was in there now; I could hear him rustling around at the far end. I started to walk around the edge of the trees, calling him.

'Fox-e-e!'

When he made no effort to come to heel I climbed the iron fence and dropped down among the brambles and nettles. It was a good deal warmer under the trees than outside, and it was absolutely quiet, not a sound except for Foxy snuffling about somewhere in the middle.

Forcing a path through tangles of briars isn't easy. They seem to reach out at you, to want to tear your clothes as you pass. The trees there are very close together, small saplings with green trunks. It is damp, and the ground underfoot is wet and mossy.

'Fox-e-e!' I called.

It was then that I discovered the cottage. One moment the trees were very close together, and the bramble bushes were thick; the next minute I found myself in a large clearing facing a ruined, derelict building. It was only a small place, a deserted red-brick house with four empty windows that stared down at me. But the roof was still on, and the black front door hung sideways on a single hinge. I thought when I first saw it that it looked a mysterious place, and I have often wondered since who lived there and how it came to be empty and neglected and forgotten.

I went to the entrance and looked in. A narrow staircase led upstairs. To the right and left there were two small rooms, and at the back was a stone-flagged scullery. The wooden floorboards were missing in some places, and the staircase railing had gone.

I decided to go inside; you would have done the same. The room on the right had a small fireplace full of bricks and rubble, and there was very little plaster on the ceiling. Someone had lit a fire in the middle of the floor and there were old, yellow newspapers lying around. In the other front room I disturbed a black-bird, which flew noisily out of the window. The place was very dirty and damp. In the scullery there was an old sink full of leaves, but the tap worked. The yard at the back was wild with golden rod and thistles and dockweed, and there was a broken-down pig sty near the house.

Then I went upstairs, treading carefully because the stairs were rotten. Here there were two small bed-rooms and a tiny passage, but only one room had a fireplace. The wallpaper had long since peeled away, leaving the plaster yellow and bare. There was straw in a corner of one room, as if someone had slept there. I rubbed the window-pane over with some straw and looked out and saw Foxy sitting on his haunches in front of the house, gazing up at me.

'Come on here, you silly old thing!' I called.

He gave a little yelp, jumped to his feet and came running up the stairs to greet me.

'What do you think of it?' I asked, but I needn't have bothered, he was as intrigued as I was by the cottage. First he ran all around the rooms sniffing in corners and standing up with his front paws on the sills to try to look out of the windows. Then he examined the overgrown garden and pig sty.

It was, I decided, our own private mystery cottage, and we would keep it to ourselves.

Chapter Two

I borrowed the yard broom when there was no one around, and took a hammer and nails from the barn and went down to the cottage with Foxy to carry out some repairs and clean the place up. It took me all Sunday afternoon, and even then I could only get one of the chimneys clear, there was so much rubble. But I lit a fire and burned the straw, and Foxy and I sat down on a log in front of the fire, and it was quite cheerful there, in the small front room, with the blaze roaring away. Foxy lay down and went to sleep with his head between his paws.

Later that week I took some provisions down to the house, in case of an emergency; a drinking bowl and plate for Foxy, candles in case we wished to stay after dark, brown paper which I nailed over the empty window-frames to keep out draughts, a tin to store food in, and some extras such as matches, a torch and a bucket. All these things I borrowed from Mum, who understood from the first that I had a secret retreat. But of course she was used to it; a year earlier, when the cub was very small, I had made a house of my own up in the Great Wood, where we had spent our summer afternoons building up the walls and roof with boughs and leaves, until finally you couldn't see a glimmer of outside light, once you were in and the torch was switched on.

The trouble was that it got damp when it rained, and we had to give it up. But the house in Gipsy Wood was much better, and except for one place where there were some missing tiles, the roof was almost perfect.

We spent nearly every Sunday afternoon in the cottage, cleaning it up and making it nicer to live in. On Saturday afternoons we usually play cricket, but Foxy is rather a nuisance, he keeps running after the ball. Once he got away with it and we all had to chase him around the pond until Charlie unexpectedly caught him by the tail and we forced the ball out of his mouth; even then he didn't want to give it up. There is always a risk that if you hit a four Foxy will be on the boundary first, the most eager fielder in the game, waiting to run off with the ball. It's a nuisance when you're in the middle of a game.

'What on earth do you do with yourself on Sunday afternoons?' asked Dad one evening, when I was helping feed the chickens.

'Nothing much,' I said. Sometimes you have to keep your secrets to yourself, you can't share them. Foxy sat by the water tap and gave a little yawn, as if to say that he knew. But I thought it wiser not to tell, in case Dad decided that the house wasn't safe, or that he had other ideas of how I should spend Sunday afternoons. Just suppose the wood belonged to someone, and I was trespassing? You could never be sure. So I kept quiet.

Later that evening I got a surprise. Just after supper, which we always have in the parlour, sitting around the big oak table, Mum said, 'David, I want you to come down to Mrs Whiteways with me after school tomorrow. It'll only take about an hour.'

'Whatever for?' I asked. The Whiteways are those awful shooting people I told you about, and Mrs Whiteway is the worst of the lot. I could think of a million ways I'd rather spend an hour than with *her*. I expect my face must have shown it, I'm not very good at hiding my feelings.

'You needn't look like that,' said Mum. 'She has her nephew staying with her and she asked if you could meet him.'

'Why?' I asked. 'What's wrong with him?'

'Nothing. He doesn't know anyone in the village, and he wants someone to show him around, and play with him.'

'How old is he?'

'About your age, dear. You must be nice to him.'

'Will he come to school?'

'No, he goes to one in Switzerland.'

It seemed a long way to go to school, but I didn't say anything; sometimes you know that you must do what you're asked. So I just nodded, and wondered what Mrs Whiteway's nephew would be like. Not as big and ghastly as she was, I hoped. And next day, after school, I met Mum by the post office and we walked across the green to the gates of the big house where the Whiteways live.

I'd never been inside, and it all seemed large compared with the farm. The house was long and low, but I didn't think the Tudor beams looked real. You could have put the whole of our place into the garden, barn and all, and there was a little stream running through the centre, with bridges you could walk over and goldfish swimming in pools and plaster kingfishers and some stone rabbits. It was lucky we didn't bring Foxy, he would have gone straight into the stream and probably tried to attack the imitation rabbits. There was also a smashing swimming pool with blue tiles, that looked as if no one swam in it.

The front door was so tall that you could have ridden our pony through it. It was like one of the doors at Arundel Castle. But it didn't look really *old* to me, everything seemed imitation, as if the builders had been asked to make it ancient, using new material.

Mum pulled on a long black iron handle by the side of the door and a bell tinkled in the distance. We waited for ages, but at last we heard footsteps and a butler in a black suit opened the door. I'd seen him before in the village, coming out of the White Lion, but I hadn't known who he was. He looked frightfully superior, as if we should have gone round to the back. Perhaps we should.

'Mrs Whiteway?' said Mum.

'What name shall I say?' He didn't smile or anything, his face just stayed dull. But I don't remember that I've ever seen him smile. He looked like the kind of butler you see on the pictures, or the telly.

'Mrs Hedger?' said Mum.

'Please come in. Medem won't be long.' He didn't say Madam, he said *Medem*. Fancy calling Mum *that*!

He showed us into a long room with the biggest blue and gold carpet I'd ever seen, and lots of polished furniture like you see in the Lewes and Brighton antique shops. There were a whole lot of stuffed birds in a big glass case – blackbirds and pheasants and a falcon – and I wondered if Mr Whiteway had shot them. One of the blackbirds was only a baby. There was a kestrel, too.

Suddenly the door opened and in came Mrs Whiteway, followed by a weedy little boy of about nine who looked as if he needed a good wash behind the ears.

'So nice of you to come, Mrs Hedger,' she said. She was wearing a pair of checked black-and-white trousers which were much too tight. Her face was very heavily made-up, and she wore long black eyelashes that didn't look at all real.

'This is Clarence,' she said, and I almost felt sorry

for him. There are so many names you can choose, like Bill or David or John or Peter or Jeremy or Paul or Richard – or even Ringo – that it just seems impossible that anyone could actually call a fellow *Clarence* and not expect to get a laugh. But I must say the name somehow suited him, he looked quite goofy standing there staring at us from behind his magnifying spectacles. They made his eyes look ridiculously big, like a goldfish in a tank.

Mum said, 'David's going to take you out and show you around, and introduce you to his friends.'

Well, I wish she hadn't said it. Directly I heard her, I knew it would be disastrous. You can't force people to get to know others, and couldn't imagine Charlie or Sue or any of my other mates taking to this funny-looking boy. It was going to be rather difficult. Then Clarence opened his mouth and spoke.

'Can we go shooting?' he asked.

As you can imagine, I nearly fell over backwards. It was just about the last thing I wanted to hear.

'Of course you may,' said Mrs Whiteway. 'You can try out your new gun up in the woods. It's only an airgun, but it's quite accurate. He's a good shot.'

Mum didn't say anything. I guess she knew what I was thinking. I daren't look at her.

'And can we go hunting?' asked Clarence.

Well, that did it. I felt like exploding, and I knew I'd gone red in the face. 'Hunting *what*?' I asked, not daring to look at Mum.

'Foxes,' said Clarence.

I said, slowly, 'As a matter of fact I've got a tame fox of my own, so we don't hunt. But don't let me stop you if you want to.' I made it sound as if hunting was quite the end, which it is. 'Anyway, hunting doesn't start until the autumn.'

'Why don't you come up to the farm tomorrow morning?' said Mum, and of course they agreed, and I knew I wasn't going to get a free weekend for quite a while.

'How long are you staying?' I asked, as they saw us to the door.

'Until my people come back from their cruise,' said Clarence. 'About a month.' I didn't bother to mention it, but I could understand why they hadn't taken him with them.

That Saturday was one of the most ghastly days of my life. Clarence arrived just after breakfast with his beastly airgun.

'Is that your fox?' he asked, the most stupid question I've ever heard. Foxy certainly didn't look like a pussy cat lying on the lawn.

'Come on, boy,' said Clarence, and Foxy jumped up and began to paw at him, anxious to be friendly.

'Oh, go down,' said Clarence and drew away.

'You needn't be afraid,' I said. 'He's quite tame.'

'I'm not afraid. I just don't like animals touching me. They're dirty.'

'Not Foxy,' I said.

'What shall we do, then?' he asked.

'Shall we go up to the wood on the hill?' I suggested. 'You get a good view of the village from up there.'

'I'll bring my gun,' said Clarence.

'Better not. You're not really meant to shoot up there.' It wasn't true, of course, the beastly Whiteways often went banging away in the wood. I added: 'But let's take the field-glasses out of the hall.'

Foxy knew at once where we were going and he was off in front of us, racing away through the farmyard and along the footpath towards the Great Wood. The view from the wood is smashing. Down below the hill you can see the village stretching out like a map, with everything clearly marked. There is the main road, narrow and twisting, running along past the houses and shops and hedges and green fields towards Horsham; farther on there are farms and barns and woods which seem quite close, once you watch them through the field-glasses. I could even see Mr Outen the postman riding on his bicycle past the village pond; the vicar's wife was hanging out washing in her garden; Mr Norwell's cows were all lying down at the end of the buttercup meadow – a sure sign of rain; I handed the glasses to Clarence.

'Have a look round,' I said. 'Foxy! Where are you?'

He gave a little yelp, he was digging a big hole

nearby; the earth was flying up behind him in great chunks.

'Do all the woods have names?' asked Clarence.

'Most of them.'

'Then what's that one called?'

'Which?'

'The one down by that stream.'

'That's Gipsy Wood. It's meant to be haunted. No one goes there.'

'Someone's lit a fire there.'

'A fire? In the wood?'

'Yes, take a look.'

He was right. Through the powerful lenses I could see the top of one of the chimneys of the secret cottage. And there was a thin curl of smoke rising from it.

'That's funny,' I said.

Now who, I wondered, could have moved into the place and set himself up with a fire? I decided that I would find out that same evening, once Clarence had gone home and the coast was clear.

I didn't get out until after tea because Mum made me help with the washing up. If there's one thing I hate it's messing about in the kitchen. Housework just bores me. So it was nearly six o'clock before I could whistle to Foxy and take his leather lead down from the hook by the front door.

'Don't be late for supper,' said Mum. 'Where are you off to?'

'A fire in the wood?'

'Oh, just down to the village,' I said, as Foxy jumped up high to grasp the lead between his teeth. 'Down, boy, down!'

I had wondered about taking him to the cottage with me, but he was so eager to go I couldn't refuse. By the time we reached the pond I had regretted my decision because there was a good deal of traffic along the narrow lane and he kept pulling on the lead. Worse, just as we reached the old blacksmith's shop it started to rain. And by the time we got to the edge of the wood it was coming down quite fast.

There was no one around. A June evening in Woodmere is pretty quiet once you get away from the main road, and down there by the wood I could hear only the birds and, far away in the distance, the sound of the Horsham train rolling along between the meadows. Not that we were really alone, because long before we reached the edge of the wood I could see the thin waft of smoke rising above the trees. Our visitor was still in the cottage.

It's a bit of a nerve, I thought. After all, I'm the one who cleaned the place up and did the repairs and made it comfortable. But I was curious to see exactly what kind of stranger we had attracted.

You simply can't help making a noise in that wood, the twigs snap under your feet, and there are so many brambles that you have to keep stopping to disentangle yourself. I let Foxy off the lead, but this was a mistake, because he made even more noise than I did, scurrying to and fro among the undergrowth and making little whimpering noises, just as if he had never been there before.

'Oh, do shut up,' I whispered.

It was tough going, but presently we came out into the clearing and stood looking at the cottage. Nothing appeared to be changed since I was last there except for the rising chimney smoke. But then everything suddenly started happening at once.

'Hi!' shouted someone from the bedroom window, and a moment later a shaggy dog came rushing out of the front door straight towards us. For a second I didn't know what to do. He was making such a terrible growling noise that I felt like running. If I'd had time to climb up the nearest tree, or had thought of it, I daresay I would. But what about Foxy, only a third of the size of this fierce thing, standing there waiting? I pulled his lead from around my neck and started forward towards the oncoming, growling dog.

'Get back, go on, get back!' I shouted, waving my arms about.

To my relief, the shaggy creature suddenly stopped when he was almost on us, and began to bark fiercely, the loudest and ugliest noise I've ever heard. Foxy whimpered and moved a little closer to me.

'Go on! Get back, you brute!' I shouted, waving my arms again. But before I realized what was happening Foxy had leaped at the dog and they were grappling together on the ground, the dog snarling savagely, the fox yelping and snapping, first one on top, then the other, over and over, a flurry of fur and waving feet and biting teeth.

I knew it was dangerous to interfere in dog fights, but somehow this was different. Foxy is really no fighter and his opponent seemed so vicious that the conflict was bound to end in disaster. So I waved the leather lead high and brought it down *smack* on top of them both.

'Stop it, you two!' I shouted. 'Stop fighting!' And I cracked them again with the lead. It seemed the only thing to do. But still they went sprawling on, yelping and snarling and struggling to tear at one another with angry jaws. Then, unexpectedly, it was suddenly all over and they were separated, standing apart, both covered with water and shaking themselves. And next to me, holding an empty bucket – *my* bucket – stood a tall thin boy. I'd say he looked about sixteen, and he was wearing blue jeans and an open-necked white shirt with a camera hanging around his neck. He just stood there, grinning, with a great mop of fair hair hanging over his eyes, while the dog and Foxy ran around trying to get dry. They both looked quite thin, with their coats all wet.

'Thanks,' I said.

'It's the only way,' he said. 'I expect Judy thought you were coming to attack us. You can't blame her really, she was protecting me. She probably thought your dog was – my goodness, it isn't a dog, is it? It's a fox. That's a bit odd, isn't it?'

'He's tame,' I said.

'I'll take your word for it. Look what it's done to Judy's ear. Come here, girl.' And to my surprise, when the dog crept forward towards her master I saw that her left ear was bleeding. I was sorry, of course, but secretly rather proud of Foxy.

'Never mind,' said the boy. 'Your fox is limping.'

He was right. Foxy's front left paw had received a nasty bite, and he seemed to be in pain.

'We'd better go inside,' said the boy. 'There's a tap in the kitchen.'

'I know,' I replied.

'Oh, you've been here before?'

'Often. I didn't think anyone else knew about it.'

'So it was you who left the candles and the torch and the other things?'

'And the bucket,' I said.

'Useful,' he said.

We had reached the doorway and the dog began to growl. The boy bent down and patted her on the head.

'None of that,' he said. 'You just behave yourself. Let's go upstairs.' And although the dog didn't seem very happy at our intrusion, she didn't make another murmur, but trotted obediently behind her master.

He had laid a sleeping bag out on the floor over a groundsheet, and the place was cleaned up.

'Have you been here long?' I asked.

'Two days. I'm walking to Dorset, to the bird sanctuary.'

'What for?'

'To see if I can get a job. I've just left school. My parents have gone to Switzerland, and I've got an uncle down in Dorset.'

'It's a long way to walk,' I said.

'I've got plenty of time. I may stay on here for a few days. Would you hold Judy still while I bathe her ear?'

The dog was thinner and smaller than I had thought, and she had bright eyes and a swishy little tail. She kept quite still while I held her, and didn't even whimper when the boy wiped her ear with his handkerchief dipped in water. Foxy sat down and watched us, and when we had finished I picked him up and we examined his paw. He didn't like it at all and made stupid, squealing noises. He struggled when we started to clean his paw and it took both of us to hold him.

'We'd better tie it up with the handkerchief,' said the boy. It was easier said than done; Foxy wasn't half as brave as Judy. But at last the job was finished, and he struggled free and limped away to the corner of the room where he lay down and looked up at us with large amber eyes full of disapproval. Sometimes I think Foxy is terribly sloppy.

'What's your name then?' the boy asked, handing me a towel to dry my hands.

'David,' I said.

'Mine's Geoffrey. I'm fifteen.'

'I'm twelve. Next birthday, that is.'

We shook hands. I felt I had found a friend, someone who liked the countryside, and was experienced
with animals.

Chapter Three

Next day was a Sunday so we spent the morning out together in the woods towards Horsham, and at midday we went swimming in the mill pond. Geoffrey hadn't brought swimming trunks with him but Charlie lent him a pair and the three of us dived in together and went splashing around, and then we lay out to dry in the sunshine on the grass bank. Foxy and Judy were becoming quite used to one another, and there was no longer any growling. In fact they seemed quite contented to sit and guard the clothes while we swam.

It was one of those warm June days when Woodmere is at its best. All around the banks of the pond the mosquitoes were buzzing and the swallows were swooping low to catch them; the pond was so still you could make ripples as you swam, circles that spread out wide across the surface of the water; you couldn't even hear the traffic on the main road; when you lay on your back and floated, the sky above was perfectly blue.

Charlie didn't really understand Geoffrey; he probably hadn't met anyone like him before. If you live in a little community like ours people seem much the same, but a stranger suddenly arriving strikes you as out of the ordinary. I had already discovered that Geoffrey was quite different. For one thing, he sounded better educated than most of us. For another, he was more energetic. Whereas Charlie and the rest of the boys were used to sitting around taking life easily, Geoffrey liked getting things done.

'Well, what are you going to do on this 'ere walking tour?' asked Charlie. 'Why don't you go by train or bus, or get a motorbike?'

Geoffrey said, 'I'd much rather walk, or hitch-hike. It doesn't matter how long it takes to get there. I could stay a day or three or four days, if I want to.'

'But wouldn't anyone mind – at home?'

'Oh no, I've tamed them. They're used to me. No problems there.'

'What about money?' I asked. 'I mean, you've got to eat.'

'I'm pretty careful. It's surprising what you can do if you don't rush out and spend all your cash on the first day. Besides, travelling costs nothing. I either walk or hitch-hike. If I get to my uncle's some time next week or the week after, it won't matter. I'm not in a hurry. I like seeing places.'

'You mean you want to be a tramp, or a beatnik?' said Charlie.

'I don't want to be anything,' said Geoffrey. 'I just want to be myself, not to be put into a kind of pigeon-hole labelled whatever-it-is. I think I *might* be a gardener, one day. It's best outdoors, out in the open, that's what I like. I wouldn't want to work in an office, or a factory or a shop – would you?'

I didn't say anything; it was all right for me because I live on a farm and I suppose one day I may be a farmer. But Charlie's dad is the local butcher and as sure as our old church clock is always slow, so Charlie will one day stand in that same unhealthy, old-fashioned little shop near the green, cutting up meat and chopping at bones.

'Well, what's wrong with a shop?' asked Charlie. 'It's good money, isn't it?'

'Money?' replied Geoffrey. 'Whoever said anything about money? I was talking about being happy enjoying yourself.'

Charlie said, 'Well, it's easier to be happy if you've got money.' Which was a funny thing to say because the only really rich people in our village are the Whiteways, and you wouldn't call them happy. Everyone knows they're always fighting. They even had a row in the post office. I reckon money hasn't done much for them, and it isn't likely to. Come to think of it, there isn't a great deal of money in our home. But we're happy, and Foxy – with only sixpence in his savings box – is probably the most contented of us all. Mum says you can't measure happiness in terms of pounds, shillings and pence.

Charlie said, 'But isn't there something you'd like to be?'

Geoffrey said, 'I wouldn't mind being a vet. We've got a white cat at home and someone threw a brick at it and broke in its face. Then they drove off in a car. I suppose they were mad, you must be crazy to do a thing like that. Our cat was in a terrible state, we couldn't get it out of the hayloft. We thought we'd have to put her to sleep, but the vet came and patched her up and set her jaw bone, and after a fortnight she got well. No one but a good vet could have done that. It's pretty fabulous work. Like being a doctor.'

'We've got a dog at home,' said Charlie. 'And some hens.'

'I've got a pony,' said Geoffrey. 'Have you ever been riding?'

'No,' said Charlie.

'Nor me,' I said. 'The mare on the farm is still too large. But I expect I'll ride her one day.'

'It's a wonderful way of getting around,' said Geoffrey. 'If I had a proper horse I'd have brought it with me. The traffic spoils riding, but if you go up on the Downs you can get right away from the mob and go right into Hampshire. And Dorset is fairly unspoiled. You see an awful lot from the saddle.'

I envied him, he was so grown-up, and he obviously enjoyed life and made the most of it. Lying there in the sun while the swallows swooped low around us, and Geoffrey went on talking about his pony and the cats they had back home, I began to wonder what I was going to be when I grew up. Would I be a farmer, like my foster father, or would all the countryside have vanished by then, giving way to new towns and broader roads and housing estates? I would be sorry if that happened. Since I had left the orphanage in London I had learned to like the green fields around Woodmere, and to be at home in the woods where the rooks live high up in the trees and the rabbits come out at night and play on the edge of the fields.

'I like taking photographs, too,' said Geoffrey. 'I've got some smashing pictures of birds on their nests, but you have to be patient.'

When we had dressed we all walked over to the mill and Geoffrey went with us up the lane towards the green.

'You be all right for food?' asked Charlie, as I stooped to put Foxy on the lead.

'Sure, I've got several tins,' said Geoffrey.

'I'll bring you some bacon in the morning, if you want.'

'Thanks very much, I'd like that.'

' 'Bye, then.' We turned away and left our new friend standing by the stile, with Judy sniffing around in the hawthorn hedgerow. I turned back when we got to the bend in the road, but they had gone.

'Funny thing,' said Charlie. 'Did you notice his shoes?'

'Not really. What about them?'

'They weren't country shoes. Not strong, not the

kind you'd wear if you were going on a long walk to – wherever he said he was going.'

'Dorset. That's the other side of Bournemouth.'

'But he was wearing quite light shoes.'

'Perhaps he hasn't any thick ones,' I said.

Charlie looked thoughtful. 'I'll tell you another thing,' he said, as we passed the pond.

'What?'

'He knew where he was.'

'What do you mean?'

'When I said we ought to go swimming it was him that mentioned the old mill pond. If he's a stranger then how did he know about it?'

I said, 'He's been here several days. It isn't far from the cottage.'

'What cottage?'

Help, I thought, I've given the game away. Not even Charlie knew about my secret hideout. I hadn't told a soul. He had supposed Geoffrey was sleeping out in the open somewhere, and we hadn't mentioned the house in the wood.

'Oh, it's nothing, really,' I said, and thank goodness he didn't go on about it.

'I was wondering if I ought to start a new gang,' he said.

It was quite an honour to be asked to join one of Charlie's secret societies, although they came and went rather quickly. Some lasted a few weeks, others only a couple of days. There had been the Red Circle

Gang, when we all wore a mysterious mark on our right arms — a circle of blood, Charlie called it, but it was really red ink. That lasted about three weeks. Then there was the Black Hand Gang, with a secret meeting place over by Hovenden's farm. This ended quite suddenly when old Mr Hovenden discovered his plum orchard had been raided. In that gang we all had dirty right hands and clean left hands, but as a badge it was a failure. Miss Thring noticed from the first day that something was wrong; half her arithmetic exercise books were covered with grimy thumbprints and smudges. She made us go out and scrub our hands clean. After which, as Jimmy Norwell said in the wash-house, Charlie had better think up some new ideas.

'And they'd better be good,' said Jeremy.

The difficulty was to find a new kind of secret society, something attractive which didn't need too much work and whose rules weren't too difficult or unpleasant. Gangs which had special ceremonies, like drinking ink or painting your toenails green, just weren't popular. Charlie had tried them all.

'You'll have to think of something good,' I said, as we came to his father's shop. 'Not like that time we had to wear one white and one grey sock.'

Charlie grinned. 'I'll tell you when I've thought about it a bit more,' he said. 'This time we'll have a really smashing gang.'

*   *   *

Next day, at breakfast, things really began to happen. I was down before Mum finished laying the table in the kitchen, and I'd almost finished my cornflakes when Dad arrived.

' 'Morning,' he said, picking up the newspaper and sitting down in his tall-backed chair. He never says much at breakfast, but today he was quite talkative.

'I went to have a look at the chickens,' he said. 'They were making the devil of a noise at about three this morning. Someone – or something – has been there.'

'Any damage, dear?' asked Mum.

'They were all shut away, but something's got in under the wire. Something quite big, like a fox.'

I went on eating my cornflakes and kept my eyes fixed on the plate. A fox, had he said?

'There was earth scraped up under one of the huts,' said Dad. 'If any of the birds hadn't been locked up we'd have lost them. It made quite a hole under the wire fence.'

I said, 'It couldn't have been a fox, or it would have made just a small hole, or jumped over the top.'

'Well, no damage done,' said Mum. But walking down the lane to school half an hour later, I wasn't so happy about the situation. If a fox had really invaded our chicken run then sooner or later Dad would be out there with a gun, to prevent a daylight raid while the old hens were innocently pecking about in the open.

And I couldn't help feeling that the fox, no matter what it was like, was really a friend – and perhaps even a relation – of Foxy's. There wasn't any doubt that any fox which came down from the Great Wood, where I had found my cub, was in some way related to Foxy, one of the family. Besides, I like foxes – tame or wild – and I understand them.

I was thinking also that a fox which came in so close to the farm must be hungry, probably lean and thin, with a rough coat and wild eyes – not at all like my well-groomed, tame fellow sleeping at home curled up in his basket in the kitchen. Foxy is always well fed and cared for. Pity the four-footer who isn't so lucky. But don't shoot him, I thought, don't shoot him. No fox is as bad as that.

I was thinking over the problem during the morning geography lesson, while Miss Thring was explaining about the industries of England. Sometimes she goes on rather a lot, and her voice gets monotonous, so you yawn and want to go to sleep, or your thoughts turn to more interesting things, like flying in a glider plane, or swimming in the sea at St Ives, which we did last year on holiday. I like Miss Thring, but I don't care much about geography, and I was quite enjoying myself, wondering how Sue had managed to plait her long hair like a horse's tail, when I suddenly realized everyone had gone silent. There wasn't a sound in the room and Miss Thring was looking straight at me.

'David!' she exclaimed.

'I'm sorry,' I said. 'I didn't quite . . .'

'You're dreaming!' she said. 'You were miles away! Very well, I will repeat the question and we shall see how much you have learned.' Miss Thring always talks like that, very precise, as if everyone is barmy.

'Yes,' I murmured.

'Kindly tell the class what Luton is famous for. Luton – just here.' And she pointed with her ruler to a black spot on the map which I'd never even seen before.

I hadn't any idea, and yet I didn't like to say so. Luton, Luton, I thought. It was a funny name but I couldn't connect it with anything. All sorts of ideas went floating through my mind, but I couldn't for the life of me remember, if I had ever heard, what Luton is noted for. What made it so famous? Fireworks? Sausages? Motor-cars? Space rockets? Boots and shoes? No, that was Northampton.

'Come along now, David.' The trouble is that once Miss Thring gets her teeth into anything she won't let go. Sue turned her head slightly towards me and whispered something, but I couldn't hear what she said, it sounded like 'cats', yet that was absurd. All towns have cats, and I don't suppose Luton has more than the others. I glanced quickly around the classroom, but it didn't help. Furniture? Clocks? Books? Desks? Blotting paper?

'Tell him please, Norwell,' said Miss Thring.

Jimmy Norwell shot up out of his seat like a rocket and said loudly, 'Straw 'ats!'

I could hardly believe it. All that fuss about some measly straw hats. Nobody in Woodmere wears one, not even old Mr Tidy, whose clothes are almost prehistoric.

Miss Thring said, 'Pay more attention, David, unless you wish to stay in after school.'

After that I had to settle down and listen to her dreary long recital of cities and towns and industries. Nottingham for lace, Reading for biscuits, Glasgow the biggest port in Scotland, Coventry for cars, and so on. I was terribly bored. But by the time the bell rang for the dinner break, and we all went running and laughing and whooping out into the field behind the school, I had made up my mind. I would go out that night, when everyone was asleep, and find out for myself exactly what kind of creature had dared to invade our chicken run. Was it really a wild fox?

Luckily, the moon was almost full. I lay in bed until I heard Mum and Dad come upstairs and shut their door. Then I pushed back the bedclothes and sat on the end of the bed looking out of the open window. Above the sill I could see the slate roof of the barn, greyish blue in the moonlight. Somewhere in the farm buildings I heard one of the cows stir restlessly. Probably Daisy, I thought. She's going to have some calves pretty soon.

Without moving from his warm position, curled up on my bed, young Foxy lay watching me, and I bet he was wondering what was going on and what would happen next. But if he thought he was going out, he was wrong.

'Listen, you,' I whispered. 'You can't come. It's too risky. You stay here on guard. Right?' And to make sure he understood, I patted the top of his head. He opened his mouth, gave a little yawn, and settled down with his nose well into the blankets.

'And don't dare move!' I added.

It didn't take long to dress, I simply pulled a jersey over my pyjama jacket, slipped into some old jeans, and pulled on my rubber shoes. Then I stuffed my dressing-gown into the bed so it looked like someone asleep. Finally, I took my pocket torch down from the top of the bookshelf and quietly opened the bedroom door. Sometimes it squeaks, so I had to be careful. But this time it didn't make a sound.

Creeping downstairs was more dangerous because the old stairs squeak and creak, and I had to stop twice, in case anyone stirred. I could feel my heart beating fast; I'd never gone out at night on an adventure of my own. I hoped Foxy wouldn't get restless, and start waking up the household, or I might be discovered.

The grandfather clock in the hall ticked almost as loudly as my heart. I went into the kitchen and through to the larder in search of some food to take with me. Supposing I was out there for a few hours, I might need something to eat. There was half a ham on a plate under a wire cover, and a big round smelly cheese, and eggs, lettuces, a cucumber and tomatoes. There was also, close to the window, a small piece of cold beef which had been left over from supper. I thought I couldn't offer cheese and lettuces or cucumber to a hungry wild fox, but beef would go down well. So, feeling rather guilty, I reached out my hand and slipped the meat into the back pocket of my jeans.

It wasn't as difficult as I had expected. I just had to let myself out, cross the farmyard, and lift the latch of the wooden gate to slip inside the chicken run among the long rows of dark huts. Inside, the chickens would all be perched up on their shelves, fast asleep. I hoped Foxy was also asleep, back on my bed.

Now I was faced with the difficulty of finding out exactly where the midnight visitor had crept under the wire. I walked around inside the fence, shining my torch. It isn't easy to discover fox marks at night under a wire fence, and there were several places where he might have broken through. The fence was a good deal taller than I, and closely meshed, but if a fox had really wanted to get into the chicken run he could have climbed over the top. I've seen Foxy scramble over quite a high brick wall, rather like a cat. But at last I found what I thought looked like the place, where the earth was disturbed and there was quite a big hole under the wire netting. Such a large hole, in fact, that I began to doubt if a fox had really made it.

I sat down against the nearest shed, and waited. I could feel the piece of beef in the back of my jeans and I wished I had wrapped it in paper, to prevent a stain. Exactly how long I sat there I don't know, because I must have dozed off, but as I said to Charlie later, when I was telling him the story, out in the playground, it was so quiet there, and there wasn't even a rustle from the wood beyond the fence, not a sound. So you couldn't really blame me for falling asleep when I was tired.

I was dreaming, too, and yet I knew it was an impossible dream. Foxy had run off up to the Great Wood and couldn't be found, and the boys from the school led by Charlie and Sue and Jeremy, had formed a search party and were out looking for him. As they walked forward through the wood they held out small pieces of beef, to attract him. I knew all the time it was only a stupid dream, I reckon I was half asleep. And then suddenly I woke up.

The wire in front of me was rattling and I realized with a thrill of alarm that my visitor had arrived. The wild fox was forcing its way under the wire. But was it really a fox? I sat quite still, waiting and listening and wondering. It was too dark to see anything, but I was wide awake now and anxious to discover exactly what the creature looked like. Yet I didn't dare switch on my torch for fear of frightening him.

First there was a twanging on the wire, then a strange grunting and snuffling. I kept quite still, aware that the slight wind was blowing straight towards me and that whatever it was couldn't smell me. Then came a series of little grunts and I sensed that the arrival was quite close. I raised my right hand holding the torch, pressed the button, and the strong beam of white light suddenly fell on a large black and white face, something much bigger than I had expected. Black it was, but it had a broad white streak down the centre, white sides, small, white ears, and eyes like those of a dog. It looked straight at me, as if hypnotized by the light. The two eyes flashed at me; there was quick scuffling, and then the creature's big dark furry body turned away and it was gone.

I was so surprised that I didn't collect my wits until it was all over and the animal had vanished. I'd never seen anything quite like it before, it seemed more like a small bear than a fox, and its appearance and disappearance had been so unexpectedly sudden that it was a moment before I was able to jump to my feet. Too late then to give chase, he would be far into the wood. So I turned back towards the house, and slowly made my way across the farmyard to the front door. It was only when I had reached the top of the stairs, taking each step slowly and silently, that I realized that the piece of beef in the back of my jeans was all squashed up flat. Heaven knows what Mum would say if she found it, or noticed the mark. But once inside my bedroom, the problem was solved. Foxy jumped up to greet me, and almost at once he snatched the meat from my hand.

'Good boy,' I whispered. And as he lay on the bed and started to eat his late supper, I wondered about the strange visitor I had seen down in the chicken run.

Chapter Four

I didn't say much at breakfast. Dad was out feeding the chickens, and Mum hadn't noticed that the beef was missing. I ate my cornflakes and a boiled egg, grabbed my satchel, stuffed my exercise books into it, and kissed Mum goodbye, all in a hurry because I didn't want to be late for school. I'd been late twice that week, and if you're late you don't get a seat at the back, where you can't be seen.

Foxy was outside, curled up on the mat in the porch, his smooth red fur catching the first warm rays of morning sunshine. He looked up, wagging his brush.

'Good boy,' I said. 'I'll see you later on.' Poor old Foxy, I thought, whatever will you do while I'm away? Tame foxes are like dogs, they love being taken out on adventurous walks, but when left to themselves they just sit around and grow lazy. That's why he likes the summer holidays, when we go swimming, and discover new places. I've seen him so tired after a long day asearching that he's just flopped straight out on the kitchen floor, waiting for me to fetch him a bowl of water.

All the way down the lane I kept thinking of last

night's strange adventure. I hurried, for fear of being late, but just by the gateway that leads into the four-acre field I spied Mr Tidy's bald head bobbing about over the top of the blackthorn hedge. The old man was in the meadow, chopping away at the hedge with a hand sickle. I seldom stop and talk to him, he has a habit of wasting time which can make you terribly late. You know how *slow* some grown-ups can be. But today was different, I needed advice. And who was likely to know more about the wild creatures of the woods than Mr Tidy, who had lived in Woodmere for years and years? They say in the village that he even remembers Queen Victoria. Besides, I had a few minutes to spare.

' 'Morning, Mr Tidy,' I said.

Up popped his head. He was always anxious to have a natter.

'Arh,' he said. 'You ain't got that critter with you, then?'

'I left him at home,' I said.

'That's all right, then. That Reynard looks wild to me. Ever bit anyone, 'as he?'

'Foxy doesn't bite people,' I replied, not thinking about Mr Outen the postman. Anyway, he's only been bitten once.

'I wouldn't trust him,' he said. 'You can't tame a fox, not proper!'

'Mr Tidy,' I said. 'What animal could be dark and white, and bigger than a fox?'

'*I wouldn't trust him,*' he said

'I dunno,' he said. 'Maybe a horse.' And he thought this such a good joke that he started to laugh, which is always a nuisance with Mr Tidy because it gets him sneezing, and by the time he's found his old red handkerchief and blown his nose and dried his eyes, why, half the morning's gone.

'Ha! Ha! Ha!' he chortled. 'That's a good one! A horse!'

'Mr Tidy,' I said, leaning on the gate, so that my chin rested on the top. 'Something came into our chicken run last night, bigger than a fox, like a large dog, with a white mark down its face. I saw it. What do you think it was?'

'I give up,' he said, and started laughing again. Sometimes I could hit him quite hard, he's so stupid.

'All right,' I said. 'Never mind. I thought you knew all about things around here. But it doesn't matter – I'm late, anyway.'

That got him. I thought it would. He looked up at once, more serious. 'It wasn't a fox?' he asked.

'Dark, with a white face – not a fox.'

'Then what was it?'

I said, 'I don't know. I'm asking *you*. What kind of animal would come into our chicken run at night, if it wasn't a fox?'

'Which part of your chicken run?'

'Over on the other side of the Great Wood. The other wood – what they call Brock's Wood.'

'Then that's it,' said Mr Tidy. 'That's it.'

'That's *what*?'

'That's what I thought. It wasn't a fox come to see you, it was old Brock.'

'Who's that?' I asked. 'Who's Brock?'

'Old Brock the badger. I bet that's what it was.'

'A badger!' The idea had never occurred to me, but then I hadn't lived very long in the country and I didn't know much about badgers, except that one never saw them. 'You really think that's what it was – a badger?'

'Sure. That's why they call it Brock's Wood. Brock is the old name for a badger. They've always lived up there. But I haven't been near the place for years, it's too tangly for me.'

'Yes, it could be,' I said.

'That's what it was, I'd say. I couldn't be dead certain, not having seen it myself. There *used* to be badgers up there when I was a boy. Not that we saw much of them, they generally comes out at night.'

'Thanks very much, Mr Tidy,' I said. And as I hurried off down the lane towards the school I wondered if he were right. I had a fair idea what a badger looked like – large and dark, with a white streak on his head, and a short, stumpy tail. Were they fierce, and did they attack people? Perhaps I could discover something at school.

I was late, of course, and I had to sit near the front. Our first lesson was history, all about the Wars of the

Roses, but I wasn't very interested. It seemed to have happened so long ago, I wondered why we didn't learn more about today. Mr Jeffries, who takes the history lessons, speaks in a low, mumbling voice, and I can never get interested in what he says. But after the eleven o'clock break we had one of Miss Thring's natural-history hours, and this was different. Once we had a long talk about frogs and newts and tadpoles and afterwards Jimmy Norwell collected a whole lot from the pond and brought them up to the school in a jam jar and put them in one of the girls' washbasins. This morning's lesson was about the creatures of the seashore, which was more interesting because we don't often get to the sea, except for rare trips to Brighton or Bognor Regis in the summer. In the ordinary way I would have been keen on hearing about shrimps and razor shells and burrowing starfish and cockles and crabs. But now I was thinking about something else.

At last, when the lesson was nearly over, Miss Thring asked, 'Now, are there any questions?'

It seemed a good opportunity, so I raised my right hand.

'Yes, David Grant?'

'Could you tell us about badgers, please?'

'Badgers! We're discussing the seashore. You won't find badgers on the beach, you know.'

Some idiot at the back gave a low laugh. It sounded like Charlie. But I wasn't going to be put off.

'I thought badgers was natural history,' I said.

'What a shocking sentence,' said Miss Thring. 'Did you, indeed? Very well then, we'll see how bright you all are. We have three minutes. What do you know about badgers – Charlie Elliott?'

Poor Charlie. I couldn't see him, but I reckon he was lost.

'Come along now,' said Miss Thring. 'Badgers. Stand up and tell us about them.'

'Badgers,' said Charlie, not very sure, 'badgers is animals that creep out at night . . .'

'Where do they creep?' asked Miss Thring.

'Along the ground.'

Miss Thring made a clucking noise, rather like one of our old hens. 'Yes, of course they creep along the ground. Or, more accurately, they walk. But whereabouts? Would you expect to see one in the school-yard?'

'Oh, no. In the open, like.'

'Where exactly?'

'I dunno. I ain't actually seen one, but I'd say out in the fields.'

'How large are they?'

I turned my head and saw that Charlie had his arms wide apart. 'Oh, pretty big,' he said. 'Like a dog.'

Someone near him gave a low growl, which set some of the girls giggling.

'We haven't all day,' said Miss Thring, opening her

desk and bringing out a book. 'David Grant, take this and start reading at – let me see – page sixty-three. At the top.'

I took the book and started to read out loud:

'The badger is one of the most attractive creatures of our countryside, but he is also very shy. He enjoys the secrecy of the night, and although seldom seen by man, is one of the happiest and most contented of wild animals. To see young badgers at play is to experience a rare pleasure. They are high-spirited and jovial, and like foxes they follow well-trodden paths in search of food. It is not generally apprec – apprec – appreciated that badgers form companionships which last them all their lives. They are devoted fathers and mothers and they make excellent parents, jealously guarding their young and searching for food for them. Badgers are carnivorous, and are related to the weasel family. Quite inoffensive, they exist chiefly on roots and insects, young rabbits, mice, and if they can find them – eggs. It is strange to reflect that the cruel sport of badger-baiting was popular in Britain until the middle of the nineteenth century, not much more than a hundred years ago, when it was made illegal ...'

I was really interested, and would have continued, but the school bell rang, and Miss Thring dismissed us. I returned the book to her.

'Thank you, Miss Thring,' I said. And as I went out into the playground and took the sandwiches from my satchel I determined if possible to have another look at the badgers up in the wood. They sounded much more attractive than I had expected.

There was no moon that night. Heavy, low clouds raced low over the Downs. The farmyard lay dark and uninviting beyond my open bedroom window. But next night there was the early promise of a full moon, and at eleven o'clock, when everyone else in the house was asleep, I decided to creep out again and explore the chicken run. Perhaps the badgers would be there, looking for eggs.

I had everything ready, the torch, my jersey, jeans, and rubber shoes. So it didn't take long, when the house was quiet, to make my way downstairs, through the kitchen, and out into the yard. Foxy had wanted to come with me again, but badger-seeking wasn't for him. So I left him safely curled up on the bed. And as I crossed the farmyard and walked around the big black barn I wondered what the grown-ups would say if they knew I was out exploring, instead of being asleep in bed. They certainly wouldn't be pleased.

In the distance, somewhere up in the wood, an owl hooted. I had often heard them before, from my bed just under the window. Sometimes I had seen one, a Little Owl, swooping down at dusk in search of field mice and voles. Once I had been surprised to find a young tawny fellow sitting on a tree stump gazing at me. As I walked away the bird's head moved around, watching me, but his body remained quite still.

Now I had reached the chicken run and was walking between the black sheds to the place where the badger had come last night. There wasn't a sound in the wood beyond the wire fence but I could feel the heat of the trees wafting towards me. The moon was full and bright, and everything looked strange. Then I sat down by the chicken hut, and waited. And this time I didn't have to wait long for something to happen. Soon there was a twanging at the wire fence, and a tiny grunting noise, and I knew the badger had returned.

I sat quite still, listening. If only, I thought, I had brought some eggs to attract him. He probably wouldn't stay long if there was no food. I pointed the torch towards the wire, clicked on the switch, and sent a beam of white light straight on to two eyes and a long narrow head striped white and black. For a second the eyes gazed at me unblinkingly, then the creature turned and disappeared into the darkness. But I wasn't far behind. Jumping up, I scrambled over the wire and gave chase.

Telling the story to Sue and Charlie and Jeremy afterwards, I was never sure quite how it happened. But suddenly there was a piercing yelp at my side and something went hurtling past my legs towards the retreating badger. At first I had no idea what it was. Then my torch caught a flash of red, and I knew from his bark that it was Foxy.

'Come back!' I shouted, but it was useless. A fierce snarling match was already in progress, with the promise of a fight. I flashed the torch's long beam forward and ran between the trees to the clearing where the fox and the badger faced each other. Foxy lay crouching, his teeth bared and his fur all ruffled up. The badger, twice his size, stood only a few yards away, motionless.

'Foxy!' I shouted. 'Come here at once! Leave him alone!' But he might never have heard. He merely gave a little whimper, kept his head well down, and showed his teeth.

What could I do? It looked as if the two animals would be involved in a terrible battle, and I feared that the badger would win.

'Come here!' I shouted.

Usually, he obeys orders instantly. You simply say 'sit' or 'wait' or 'lie down' or 'quiet, boy', and he knows exactly what to do. But now I was wasting my breath. I suppose he didn't dare to turn away, in case the enemy attacked. One quick leap, and the badger would have him by the neck.

In an emergency you have to make up your mind and act quickly, right or wrong. No use standing around while the house burns down or a pram starts running away. So I ran forward, waving my torch at the badger, shouting, 'Go on! Go home, you big monster!'

The badger bared his teeth, snarled, and then unexpectedly turned and *raced* away into the darkness. Foxy, with a yelp of victory, followed him.

'Come here!' I shouted. 'Come back at once, you wicked dog!' And this time he obeyed, creeping out into the torchlight with his brush well down, and his nose low to the ground, as if he knew perfectly well he ought not to be rampaging in Brock's Wood.

'That's better!' I said. 'Now what made you come out here, eh? I thought I told you to stay on the bed? Come to heel!'

He crept forward, crouching very low on the ground, and I could see that he looked pretty miserable. I've never willingly hit him, it is wrong to strike animals. A word of encouragement or a note of anger is usually enough. A dog, cat, a horse or a fox, they soon learn from your tone of voice. And Foxy has never been in doubt. So now, when he was ashamed, he lay down quite still with his ears low and his long muzzle resting on his front paws, and I knew I need only speak severely. That was enough.

'Bad dog!' I said.

He gave a whimper and then he turned over to his back, an old trick retained from his cub days, a plea that the mistake should be forgotten in favour of a game. He knew I couldn't resist him. He loves being petted.

'All right then, come on!' I said. And he jumped up and ran along by ~~my~~ feet as I walked up through the wood, flashing my torch at the trees. I wanted to discover where the badger had gone, and at last we came to the place. It was easy to find, well-worn paths led to a great mound under the trees where there were large holes dug into the bank, bigger than those made by rabbits or foxes. You could see quite clearly where the badgers had worn down the soil, forming their footpaths. But there was no sign of our friend. He was probably curled up several feet under the ground on which we were standing.

'Let's go home!' I said. And together we crept back through the farmyard, and went silently upstairs to bed. It was good to lie between the cool sheets and to feel young Foxy curled up around my feet. But the closeness of his body next to me, warm and soft, made me wonder about the other animal I had met, the wild creature up in the wood who really wasn't so fortunate as Foxy. I felt I wanted to know more about the badgers.

Chapter Five

'I think I know what it was,' I said at breakfast next morning.

'What was?' said Mum.

'The thing that came into the chicken run.'

Dad looked up from his newspaper, neatly folded in front of his plate of ham and eggs and tomatoes. 'It must have been something big,' he said. 'The hole under the wire was larger this morning. I've covered it over. Too big for a fox, I'd say.'

I said, 'I believe it was a badger.'

'Might have been. What makes you think so?'

'Oh, I just had a hunch,' I said. I couldn't very well admit that I'd been out two nights and had seen it going back into the wood. Foxy, resting his head against my left foot under the table, stirred restlessly.

Mum said, 'Do badgers eat beef?'

'They might do,' replied Dad. 'Why do you ask?' Help, I thought.

'Oh, I just wondered,' she said. And I didn't dare look up from my plate because I felt quite guilty. But nothing more was said about the missing meat or the badger, and if Mum had guessed where the food had gone she didn't mention it.

Out of curiosity, before going off to school, I worked out how Foxy had escaped out of my bedroom and down to the yard. He must have jumped out of the window onto the slate roof of the kitchen and then scrambled down the ivy to the ground – more like a cat than a fox.

That afternoon we had a half-holiday, so I thought I'd better not be late for school. But there was old Mr Tidy sitting on the bank by the letterbox, trying to light a dirty old pipe in the shelter of the hawthorn hedge, and I knew I'd have to stop and explain what had happened.

'It *was* a badger,' I said. 'I saw it.'

'Badger?' he said. 'Perishing things. Worse than foxes. You won't have any chickens left once they get in among 'em. They've been up in that wood for years. Someone ought to clear 'em out.'

I said, 'They haven't done *us* any harm.'

'But they will,' he said. 'You'll see. You wait. You mark my words, they'll have your chickens one of these nights.'

'We lock them up,' I said, wondering why Mr Tidy was anxious to kill all the wild creatures, rather like Mr Whiteway. But then it occurred to me that Mr Tidy sometimes did odd jobs in the Whiteways' garden. Perhaps he had inherited some of his employer's likes and dislikes. Maybe he, too, was someone who didn't really care for—

'I'd better be getting down to the school,' I said.

Then I left the old man puffing away at his pipe by the side of the road. I rather regretted that I'd told him about the badger.

I set off immediately after lunch to go and see Geoffrey in the cottage in Gypsy Wood. If he hadn't already started his long walk to Dorset I thought we might go swimming, or he could come out with Foxy. It wasn't a warm day, there was quite a wind, and the clouds were dark and low, more of an afternoon for walking than swimming. As we came near the cottage, Foxy ran ahead, and I knew from the barking that Judy had met him. When I reached the clearing in the wood the fox and the dog were running around in circles chasing each other's tails, and Geoffrey was sitting out on the doorstep hammering studs into the sole of a hefty-looking boot.

'Hullo,' he said. 'I'm just getting ready for the big trek.'

'When are you off?'

'Maybe tomorrow,' he said. 'I went over to Shipley yesterday and looked at the windmill. Have you been there?'

'Hilaire Belloc's mill?' I replied. 'Yes, Foxy and I have been there twice. Was it working?'

'Yes. I'd never seen a windmill turning. You get a fine view from the top. And there's a stream near it.'

'The Adur,' I said. 'It reaches the sea at Shore-ham.'

Geoffrey was sitting on the doorstep

I said, 'Do you know anything about wild animals?'

'What kind?'

'Badgers.'

He said, 'Yes, a little. They live in sets, usually in wooded country.'

'Sets?' I said.

'That's what they call their burrows. You usually find them on hillsides, in sandy soil. They all live underneath, whole families of them, with bedding.'

'Bedding?' I asked.

'Old leaves and bracken and hay and moss. They're very clean, but they spend all day underground and only come up at night.'

'To kill chickens?'

'Not usually. They prefer rabbits and mice and voles and insects and sometimes frogs. And worms and grubs. They don't really worry anyone. They usually use the same footpaths. We have quite a big set near us at home. I used to go up into the woods to watch them. When they're young they come out and play about when it gets dark. You have to hide in case they see you, or climb a tree. Once I waited an hour and they didn't come out. I think they must have heard me. They have wonderful hearing. If they are disturbed they all rush back to shelter and they don't come out again.'

'Don't they ever come out in the light?' I asked.

'Seldom. They're shy.'

'And do they kill chickens?'

'I don't think so – not if other food is easy to get, mice and grubs and so on. They often get blamed for killing poultry but it's usually the foxes who share their sets.'

'You mean they live side by side, the foxes and badgers?'

'Very often,' said Geoffrey.

That was strange, I thought, because it meant that some of Foxy's relations were living up in the wood with the badgers.

'One thing's rather funny,' said Geoffrey.

'What's that?'

'If you shine a torch with a red filter on to one of them, you know what he does?'

'No, what?'

'Nothing. He just doesn't take any notice.'

I wished I'd known about this before; the badger I had seen might not have run off if I'd used a red light.

'Would you like to see the badger up in our wood?' I asked.

'Yes, very much.'

That was how Geoffrey and I arranged to meet in the farmyard late that night and how we went together up into the wood to wait for the badgers. But something went wrong. It may have been the wind, which carried the noise of our approach. Or perhaps the badgers sensed that we were there, sitting under the tree with our torch glasses painted red, waiting to switch on directly something appeared. Whatever happened, we were still sitting there over an hour later, with not a sign of anything. All was quiet in the wood, all the creatures were asleep. I yawned, and felt cold.

'Let's go home,' I whispered.

'All right,' said Geoffrey.

We parted in the lane, with the promise that we would meet again next day at the old cottage.

Chapter Six

I was looking forward to meeting Geoffrey at the house but something happened to upset my plans. It was unexpected, and I couldn't avoid it. I was walking Foxy up the lane, and he was keeping to heel, just behind my feet. Usually I put him on the lead, facing the oncoming traffic on the right-hand side, but this morning there weren't any cars on the road. At least, I didn't think there were until I reached the corner near the green, when a big white car suddenly swept round the bend and nearly knocked us over. I almost tripped over Foxy as I stepped back. But I just had time to see that it was Mr Whiteway's car, with him driving.

'Hullo, midget,' said Sue, when I reached the green. They were sitting around on the grass.

I know I'm small, but I'm not *that* small, and she's no giant, anyway. So I said, 'How are the big fatties, then?' And Sue, who isn't exactly thin, took the hint and shut up.

'I'll tell you what, nipper,' said Charlie. 'You've got a problem on your hands, you have.'

'Yes?' I said.

'You know Brian Tidy?'

'With the green bike?'

'His grandad works on the roads up your way. I was round the Tidys' place last night and Brian was telling me about them badgers in your wood.'

'How does he know?' I asked.

'The old man told him. That Whiteway bloke is arranging a badger hunt. Mr Tidy's going to help him. They're going to dig them out, with dogs.'

'They can't do that,' I said.

Sue said, 'What's to stop them?'

'I will,' I said.

'And who else, nipper?' said Charlie.

'We'll have to think of something,' I said. 'We can't have Mr Whiteway up in our wood killing things.'

'What's to stop him?' asked Charlie.

'But they're not doing any harm,' I said. 'Badgers are quite—'

Sue interrupted. 'Who cares about a lot of smelly old badgers, anyway?'

'They're perfectly all right,' I said. 'They've been there years. They don't do any harm. What does Mr Whiteway want to kill them for? You can't eat badgers.'

'He'd shoot anything that moves,' said Jeremy, who had just joined us.

'Except Mrs Whiteway,' said Sue. And we all laughed, but I didn't really feel like joking, I was much too busy wondering if there was some way we could prevent the Whiteways and old Mr Tidy from killing the badgers up in the wood. It didn't seem right that they should be condemned to death for no reason at all. But the problem was – how could they be protected?

'Can't we do something about it?' I asked. 'Nobody's mad about the Whiteways, are they?'

'I ain't, anyway,' said Charlie. 'Still, what can you do? He owns half the village.'

'There are plenty of us,' I said. 'We ought to think of something.'

'No good *asking* the Whiteways not to do it,' said Sue. 'They'd just laugh.'

I said, 'When are they going to go up there?'

Charlie said, 'We'll have to find out. I tell you what. Why don't we all get together and form a gang?'

'You and your gangs,' said Sue. 'What is it this time? Everyone has to get tattooed, I suppose.'

'Or cross-eyed,' said Jeremy.

'That's stupid,' said Charlie. 'No, I mean a gang to stop the Whiteways. The Badger Gang, we could call it. How about that?'

'What's the catch?' asked Sue. 'Only boys allowed, I suppose?'

'No, we'll let you in this time.'

'Thanks very much,' said Sue.

'If we all met, and worked out a plan of campaign, we might get old Whiteway where we want him,' said Charlie. 'I owe him something for telling the copper about my bike.'

'What's wrong with your bike?' asked Sue.

'No lights,' said Charlie.

'And no brakes,' I said.

'Come to think of it, it's no bike,' added Jeremy. 'More like a load of old scrap iron.'

'Who else is going to join?' asked Sue.

'Just us,' said Charlie. 'And maybe Whiting, if he wants to. We don't want everyone. It's got to be secret.'

'Where will we meet?'

'Here, of course, on the green. We've always met here. It's nice and central.'

I said, 'I've got a much better idea. If we meet at *my* place we can get Geoffrey to help us. He knows a lot about badgers.'

'You mean up at your farm, with all those smelly old cows?' Sue sounded scornful.

'No,' I said. 'The cottage in the woods, the one I told you about.'

'Smashing,' said Charlie. 'Let's make it tomorrow. And everyone brings sixpence.'

'Whatever for?' asked Sue. 'I thought there was a catch in it. Sixpence!'

'Subscriptions, of course. You have to pay some-thing when you join a secret society. You needn't belong if you don't want to.'

'What happens to the money?' Sue is sensible, even if she is a girl.

Charlie said, 'We can decide about that later. If you don't trust me we'll make Jeremy treasurer.'

'Done,' I said, thinking that Charlie looked slightly hurt. 'Let's meet tomorrow evening at six at the old cottage in the woods.' And I explained how to get there.

We were all sitting around on the floor in the downstairs room while the log fire crackled and spat. It was a warm, fine evening and Charlie had brought some sausages – best pork, he said – and he was cooking them on wooden skewers over the flames. They looked rather smoky.

I had arrived early and explained to Geoffrey what was happening. Then Sue turned up, and Jeremy, and young Whiting, and last came Charlie with the sausages in a paper bag. Foxy sat in front of the fire hoping someone would give him something to eat. Judy lay in the doorway, her head resting on her forepaws, guarding the house.

'Are we going to wait till you've cooked them all before we begin?' asked Sue. 'I've got to be home by seven.'

'I can't do more than four at once,' replied Charlie. 'I've only got one pair of 'ands.'

'They look pretty burnt to me,' said Jeremy.

'Nourishing,' said Charlie, moving the spitting sausages into the flames.

'Well, what's the plan?' asked Sue.

'Let's have something to eat first,' said Charlie.

We were all sitting around on the floor

'I can't wait,' said Sue. 'Must be half past six already.'

'All right,' said Charlie, wearily. 'David – you start. About the badgers.'

'Right,' I said, and as the smell from the sausages drifted through the room where the six of us sat around on the floor, I told them all I knew about the wild creatures up in the wood, and about Mr Whiteway's plan to dig them out with dogs, and then to kill them. Before I had finished, Charlie had handed round the sausages and Foxy was nudging my knee, hoping for a piece.

'But can they do that?' asked young Whiting. 'I mean – aren't badgers protected or something?'

'Not as I know of,' said Charlie.

Geoffrey said, 'Are you sure the badgers haven't done any damage?'

'Positive,' I said. 'If they *had* done any damage it would be to our chicken run, and I'd know about it. The Whiteways live right down in the village, they'd never even know about the badgers if old Mr Tidy hadn't told them. Silly old poop.'

'When do you think they plan to do it?' asked Geoffrey.

'I don't know,' I replied.

'Bet it's a weekend,' said Jeremy. 'They always go shooting on Sundays. Bet it's a Sunday morning.'

'But how can we find out?' asked Geoffrey.

Then I remembered Clarence, the Whiteways'

nephew. I hadn't seen him in the village for several days, but if he was still staying at the house I might possibly be able to discover his uncle's plan.

'There's a stupid nephew who might tell us, if we don't make him suspicious,' I suggested.

'You mean that white-faced freak?' said Jeremy.

'That's right,' I said.

'You'd better see him right away,' said Geoffrey. 'Just in case they're going to do something *this* Sunday.'

'Do you think we might be able to stop them?' I asked. It seemed to me rather hopeless, just us kids sitting around in an old cottage in the woods plotting to prevent a rich, influential man from doing something that wasn't illegal.

Sue said, 'I suppose these old badgers are worth saving? I mean, why *shouldn't* they be dug up?'

'They're not doing any harm,' I protested.

'They're rather attractive,' said Geoffrey. 'And they help the farmer. They eat field mice and grubs and insects. Besides, it's mean, digging them out of their homes to butcher them.'

'What's wrong with butchering?' asked Charlie, wiping some sausage off his hands with a piece of newspaper.

'Nothing, stupid,' said Jeremy. 'But you can't eat badgers, can you?'

'Never tried,' said Charlie. 'Still, if Dave wants to keep them up in his wood, that's OK by me. It'll be one in the eye for old Whiteway.'

'But how will we do it?' I asked.

Geoffrey said, 'First you find out exactly what day and time they plan to attack. Then we'll work out a counterplan. There is one way we might stop them, with luck.'

'What's that?' asked Sue.

'I'll tell you later. When David has discovered what Mr Whiteway intends to do; so it's up to you to find out, Dave.'

It's up to me, I thought.

Chapter Seven

I didn't really want to see Clarence again, and for a long time I couldn't think of any excuse for calling on him. Then I decided that I'd get Mum to help, without her actually knowing it.

'Do you think I ought to go and see Clarence again?' I asked at breakfast next morning.

'I thought you didn't like him,' she said. 'You are a funny boy.'

'I don't much, but I suppose I *ought* to see him, sometimes.'

'Well, that would be nice of you,' said Mum. 'Why don't you take some eggs down to Mrs Whiteway?'

That was just what I wanted, an excuse to visit the house without it seeming obvious. So that evening, after tea, I walked down to the green, and rang the bell of the big front door of the Whiteways' house. A dozen fresh farm eggs ought to be acceptable, I thought. Mrs Whiteway opened the door.

'Mum asked me to bring you these eggs,' I said. 'They're fresh.'

She was wearing very tight blue trousers, which made her look fat.

'How kaind, how very kaind,' she said, and I noticed she had bright red lipstick on her lips which made her mouth look funny. 'Whay don't you come in and see Clarence?'

'Thanks very much, I'd like to.' It wasn't the truth, of course, but at least I was in the house, being led through large rooms into the garden at the back, where the lawn was neatly trimmed and there were great beds of flowers grouped around the blue swimming pool.

'Clarence!' called Mrs Whiteway. 'Here's a friend of yours to see you!'

He was standing under an elm tree aiming a catapult at one of the branches above him.

'S-sh!' he whispered, pulling the elastic sling right back.

I ran forward and shouted, 'Hullo, Clarence!' so loudly that a big blackbird suddenly flew out of the tree and went winging over the garden wall.

'Now look what you've done!' said Clarence. 'I nearly had him. I can't hit anything today.'

'David's called to see how you are, dear,' said Mrs Whiteway.

'What for?' asked Clarence, suspiciously.

'I just brought some eggs,' I said.

'Why?' said Clarence.

'From Mum,' I said, wondering how I was going to get the beastly boy alone so I could ask him about the badgers. It would have to be done very tactfully. If he suspected anything he would close up like a trap. We both knew we were really enemies.

'What a smashing pool,' I said.

'Think so?' Clarence gave me a doubtful look, wondering what I was getting at.

'It's hot,' I said.

'Then why don't you two have a swim?' said Mrs Whiteway. 'I could find you a costume.'

'I'd love to,' I said. And ten minutes later I was splashing about in the cold, clear blue water, while Clarence sat on the edge of the bath with his fat white legs dangling over the side.

'Why don't you come in?' I asked. 'It's not really cold.'

'Can't swim,' he murmured.

'You needn't go out of your depth,' I said. 'Try the shallow end.'

'I'm all right,' he replied, leaning down to dab some water on his head.

'Don't see much of you these days,' I said.

'I'm going home next week.'

'Far?' I asked, hoping it would be a long way off.

'London. I like London, there's more to do. It's dull here.'

'There's quite a lot to see, if you get around.'

'Yes?' He sounded doubtful.

'There's the windmill, and the mill stream, and there's the Roman villa.'

'Where's that?'

'Up beyond us, near the heath. You can see the

stones, and there's part of a pavement, with coloured tiles. They say if you dig there you find things. Pottery, and coins, and things.'

'Real coins?' he asked.

'Sure. Roman coins. Why don't you come up and have a look at the place?' I tried to sound casual.

'Perhaps I will,' he replied.

'Weekends are best,' I said, remembering he had only one weekend left before going home.

'I might manage Saturday,' he said.

'We're probably going into Horsham in the morning,' I said.

'I could make it the afternoon.'

'Why not Sunday?' I asked.

'I might in the morning,' he said. 'We're going out in the afternoon.'

'Not much good,' I said. 'We go to church in the morning. Still, you could go up there one evening.' I turned and splashed into the water, trying a slow breast-stroke. That might be it, I thought. Sunday afternoon they're going out. But where to? Were they planning to go up into the woods to hunt the badgers? I wondered how I was going to find out. I knew now that it wasn't Saturday or Sunday morning, because Clarence had been free to see the villa. But on Sunday he was going out. And I wondered where.

We dressed slowly, and hardly spoke. There really wasn't much to talk about. We had very little in common.

'Have you got a comb?' he asked. His hair looked awful, like a hedgehog.

'Afraid not,' I said, and even if I had I wouldn't have lent it to him. You shouldn't use other people's combs.

'I won't be a second,' he said, walking across the lawn and going indoors.

I wandered over to the pool and stood looking at the reflection of the trees in the water. The garden looked much more beautiful than ours, and I envied them the swimming pool, but I thought I'd rather live up at our farm than down here in this big house.

I was just turning away when I noticed something lying on the concrete. I had only a second to stoop and do what I wanted before Clarence came out into the garden again. He'd combed and brushed his hair flat.

'I ought to be getting back,' I said. 'Thanks for the swim. Might see you up our way one evening then?'

'Could be,' he said.

' 'Bye then,' I said. 'I'll find my way out.'

'OK.' He turned away, and when I reached the house I glanced back at him. He was searching around on the ground for something, and I had a fair idea what it was. His catapult. But I knew he would never find it, because during the brief moment before he rejoined me I had flung the thing far over the garden wall. I expect it's still there, lost and forgotten.

I walked back up the lane towards the farm, and

He was searching around on the ground for something

just by the letter box on the corner I noticed a hand-
some young speckled thrush perched in the hedgerow.
I whistled, and he cocked his head at me, and
watched. Then, as I came nearer, he suddenly spread
his wings and flew off. I was sure then that I'd been
right to throw the catapult away. Don't you agree?

'Hullo, boy,' said old Mr Tidy, popping his head over
the top of the gate. I was late for school as usual, but a
talk with the enemy was too important to miss, so I
swung my satchel on to the grass verge and sat
down.

'Going to be a hot day,' I said.

He sucked at his pipe and blew out a puff of
evil-smelling tobacco.

'Seen any more of them creatures up in your wood?'
he asked.

'Creatures, Mr Tidy?'

'Them Brocks. They badgers.'

'No, I haven't. Perhaps they've gone away.'

'Not they. The only time they go away is when you
dig 'em out. With dogs.'

'Dogs?'

'Bill Russell's terrier, and the postman's dog.
They'd get 'em out. But we got to have spades.'

'When for, Mr Tidy? When were you planning to
do it?'

'I dunno.' He scratched his head. 'It'll be Mr

Whiteway and 'is party'll arrange it. You got any spades up your farm?'

'I don't think so, not more than one. Think it might be soon, Mr Tidy? The digging, I mean.'

'Can't really say.' The old man screwed up his mouth.

I said, 'Well, I'd best be off, I'm late already.' And as I hurried down the lane towards the green I had an idea he knew a good deal more than he was prepared to reveal. Sunday would really be the only time that Bill Russell and Mr Outen would be available to handle their dogs. Bill is a big fellow who works in the quarry, and he's always there on Saturdays. His terrier is a fierce little thing, not at all friendly, with a nasty set of teeth. Remembering that Clarence had said he would be busy on Sunday afternoon I now felt reasonably certain this was the time fixed for the badger hunt. And a pretty one-sided hunt it looked like being, with men and dogs and spades against a few scared, almost helpless creatures trapped in their underground homes with no possible way of escaping.

I wondered why Mr Whiteway and old Mr Tidy and the others were so anxious to destroy the badger families. It wasn't as if the set was anywhere near the village, or the badgers were raiding chicken runs. I supposed it was just jealousy. Some people can't bear to see animals living free and happy. They have to shoot them, or put them into cages, or stick their heads on walls, or make them into rugs or fur coats. Poor badgers, I thought, I don't know how we're going to help you. But we'll try.

'Now who's free on Sunday morning?' asked Geoffrey. We were all sitting around on the floor in the cottage in the woods. Foxy lay by my feet with his head resting on my right leg. There was Charlie, Sue, Jeremy, young Whiting and Jimmy Norwell. That made seven of us. Everyone agreed to be available on Sunday morning.

'But why the morning?' asked Jeremy. 'David said they're going to do it on Sunday afternoon.'

Geoffrey said, 'That's why we'll have to get cracking on Sunday morning. Now here's what I plan. First of all, we're not going to be able to stop anyone getting up into the woods. David says Mr Whiteway rents the land. We can't keep the Whiteways away. They'll have dogs with them, and spades, and maybe guns. But without their dogs they can't do anything; they'll never dig deep enough with spades alone, so they'll have to send the dogs down, and it'll be a pretty fierce fight because the badgers will be fighting for their lives. So what we've got to do is to prevent the dogs getting into the set.'

'How on earth are we going to do that?' asked Sue.

Charlie said, 'We could get your Judy to lead them away.'

'Why don't we kidnap the Whiteways?' asked Jeremy.

'Lock them up for the day,' suggested Jimmy.

'No,' said Geoffrey. 'We don't want to arouse any suspicions. We don't want the grown-ups to know who's against them. We'll have to be more subtle than that.'

'What do you mean, subtle?' asked Charlie.

'Intelligent, more clever.'

'First of all,' said Geoffrey, 'we'll have to leave Judy here, out of sight. She'd only give us away. And you'd better lock Foxy up, David. It wouldn't be safe for him with guns around.'

Jeremy said, 'That old Whiteway would kill that fox as soon as look at him.'

'Right,' said I.

Geoffrey continued: 'So now we know there are seven of us, and no animals, and we've got Sunday morning to work in, but not later than midday because I guess someone will be up in the woods by then, with the spades and things.'

'But what are we going to *do*?' asked Sue. 'How are we going to stop the dogs clearing the badgers out?'

'We'll put them off the scent,' said Geoffrey.

'How?' asked Jeremy. We were all anxious to know.

'With aniseed. The people who don't like fox-hunting use it. They spread it around the hedges and set up a false scent, which the hounds follow. Then the fox goes free.'

'That's fine,' I said.

'And we'll do that in the morning?' asked Sue.

'Why not? I suggest we all meet here at ten on Sunday morning.'

'No,' I said. 'Make it the big barn of our farm, it's much nearer.'

Geoffrey said, 'All right, in the barn up at David's farm. We'll have an hour to spread the scent around, but we'll have to be guided by the way the wind is blowing. We'll need two sentries to stay on the edge of the wood while we're spreading the scent. Who'll volunteer?'

'I will,' said Jeremy.

'And me,' said Whiting.

Geoffrey went on: 'That's fine. If anyone approaches while we're working you blow whistles. We'll need two whistles, some rags, the aniseed, and some rope.'

'Why the rope?' asked Charlie.

'We'll have to make up a bundle of rags and dip it in the aniseed and then drag it around the fields. So the dogs really move away.'

'But where will we get the aniseed?' I asked.

'Well,' said Geoffrey, 'it's a question of money. If we could all chip in, we'll need about ten bob. We can buy it in Horsham, I expect. I could manage three or four bob. How about you, Charlie?'

'I've got a couple of bob. Two and three, I think.'

'And David?'

I said, 'I daresay I could get some from my dad.'

Jeremy said, 'I'm flat broke.'

Sue said she could afford four shillings, Whiting said he had a half-a-crown, and Jimmy produced ninepence straight away. So Geoffrey announced he would go into Horsham on Friday and buy the aniseed at a chemist's. The two sentries were to supply their own whistles, and I was to find the rope and the rags.

'Right,' said Geoffrey. 'Then we all meet at eleven at David's barn. Plimsolls, old clothes, and not a word to anyone about our plans.'

As we parted outside the cottage Geoffrey said to me, 'Whatever you do, keep Foxy tied up all day. We don't want any trouble. I'm leaving Judy here.'

She must have heard him, for she looked quite upset, standing in the doorway with her tail down. But Foxy dragged me all the way home, hungry for dinner.

Chapter Eight

I thought eleven o'clock would never arrive. I took Foxy up to the wood and he sniffed around among the badger set, putting his nose into the tunnels and making little squeaking noises. I reckon he knew they were down there, all curled up and warm.

Poor old badgers, I thought, with men from the village coming to dig you out and kill you. I hope we'll be able to stop them. Then I went back to the farm, but it was still only ten, and the farm was quiet and deserted, with the cows out in the four-acre field huddled in a corner swishing their tails to keep the flies off. But at last it was five to eleven, and I took Foxy upstairs and shut him in the bedroom. He settled down on the bed, but he didn't look pleased.

'You can't come,' I said. 'You stay here and go to sleep.'

Foxes are like cats; they soon curl up and doze off, and if they've got a comfortable bed they will sleep for hours.

I took the binoculars from the hall and went into the barn. Geoffrey had already arrived, so I showed him the rope and the rags. He was carrying the bottle of aniseed, a large glass jar.

forward and started to dig near a hole.

'I say,' said the tall thin man, 'shouldn't we put the little dawg straight in?'

'We ought to enlarge the entrance first,' said Mrs Whiteway, opening up her shooting stick, which she stuck in the ground and then sat on. 'How can you be sure there are any of them down there?' she asked. 'Suppose they've all gone?'

Mr Whiteway said, 'They won't be down every hole, but look at the flies going in and out of this one. There's certainly something down *there*.'

Clarence was walking around among the trees, and for a moment I feared that he might discover someone, but presently he moved away and sat down on a tree stump by the mound. Mr Tidy took up a spade and started to dig, rather slowly.

It was quite hot up there in the wood, and presently there was a clap of thunder over by Horsham and the rain started falling. You could hear it spattering on the tops of the trees. It grew rather dark.

Mr Whiteway wasn't doing any digging, but was walking up and down with his gun under his arm. The man who had been digging now rested on his spade. 'Hot work,' he said. 'We're not getting very far.'

'Come along,' said Mr Whiteway. 'Mustn't waste time.'

'We could do with another spade,' said the man.

'I swear I brought one up here this morning,' said Mr Tidy.

'Don't stop digging,' said Mrs Whiteway.

Clarence said, 'What will we do with them when we've got them?'

'Kill them,' replied Mr Whiteway.

'How?'

'Shoot them, or hit them on the head with a spade.'

'May I kill one?' asked Clarence.

'Certainly, darling,' said Mrs Whiteway.

'Then can we go home and have tea?'

'That's right, darling.'

'Good egg,' said Clarence.

I could see the little horror quite clearly from where I lay in the bracken. He was standing with his hands in his pockets, watching Mr Tidy dig. The dogs had settled down and were standing around Mr Outen's feet. The other man had lit a cigarette and was puffing smoke into the air.

'How far do you want us to dig?' asked Mr Tidy, who didn't seem to be enjoying himself.

'I think you've gone down far enough,' said Mr Whiteway. 'Let's try the terrier, she's the smallest. The hole looks big enough to me.'

Now if Mr Outen had been sensible and kept the terrier on the lead and taken her to the hole, all might have been well. But he foolishly made the mistake of slipping her off the lead, and of course she was away like a flash, racing through the wood in the direction of our aniseed circle.

'Hi!' shouted Mr Outen. 'Come back!' But the little terrier had already disappeared among the trees, and we never saw her again. This upset the spaniel and the mongrel Jim, who started whimpering and pulling in opposite directions.

'Whoa!' shouted Mr Outen. 'Give over!'

Too late, the big spaniel had already broken free and was racing away through the trees, trailing his lead behind him.

'What on earth's the matter with these dawgs?' drawled the tall thin man, taking a cigarette out of a gold case and lighting it. 'I must say, they're pretty extraordinary, what?'

'You can say that again,' said Mrs Whiteway.

'I must say, they're pretty extraordinary,' repeated the man.

'Perhaps they're upset by the thunder,' said Clarence.

Mr Whiteway walked over to Mr Outen and said, 'We'd better keep that dog on the lead. Bring him over to the mound.' But the mongrel wanted to join his companions and they had to drag him unwillingly to the set, where he sat down with his back to one of the holes, whining to be set free.

'What's wrong with the brute?' asked Mrs Whiteway.

'I'll soon fix *him*,' said her husband, pushing the poor dog around and forcing his head towards the hole. To be fair to him, the dog gave a few sniffs into the place where Mr Tidy had been digging, but he wasn't really interested. So he sat down again, which infuriated Mr Whiteway.

'For heaven's sake!' he shouted. 'Can't somebody do something? We're supposed to be hunting badgers! We'll never get one at this rate.'

It was really very funny. Old Mr Tidy had sat down on the mound and was mopping his face with a red handkerchief, Mrs Whiteway was poking her shooting stick into one of the holes, Clarence had started to dig in a hard, stony patch, and the two men had given up and were smoking cigarettes, while the goofy fellow was trying to persuade the remaining dog to show a little interest in the proceedings. I reckon the badgers were all asleep down below.

'What was *that*?' asked Mr Whiteway, standing quite still.

'Sounded like a whistle,' said Mr Outen.

And it was, two blasts on the whistle from Jeremy, which meant that someone was coming up from the direction of the farm.

'Boy Scouts,' said Mr Whiteway. But he had hardly uttered the words when something small and red came streaking through the wood towards the mound. I could see him quite clearly; he was racing through the trees at full speed towards us, and it wasn't until he reached the mound and the group of strangers that he suddenly stopped, surprised to see them.

'It's a fox!' shouted Mrs Whiteway.

They were all too astonished to move, and I hadn't time to consider how Foxy could have got out or what he was doing up in the wood, because I saw to my horror that Mr Whiteway had raised his double-barrel shotgun and was pointing it straight at Foxy, who was standing watching him, not fifteen feet away, a perfect target.

'Just keep still,' said Mr Whiteway, taking aim.

I suddenly felt terribly sick in my stomach, but even as I jumped up from the bracken shouting, 'Don't shoot! He's a tame fox! He's mine!' the unexpected miracle occurred and with a loud cry Geoffrey dropped from the overhanging branch straight on top of Mr Whiteway.

'Bang!' The gun went off with a loud report, but Foxy jumped straight up into my arms, and he was safe, licking my nose, pawing at my shoulders.

Mr Whiteway lay quite still on the ground, gasping for breath, while the others crowded around. All except Mr Tidy, that is, who seemed to be dazed by the shot, for he was lying on the ground hugging his leg.

'I think I've been hit!' he moaned. 'Oh dear!'

'Nonsense!' said Mr Whiteway. But it was soon obvious that the old man had been shot in his left leg, just above the ankle. He couldn't get up, but lay still on the ground while the others crowded around.

'What – the devil – does this mean?' gasped Mr

'It's a fox'

Whiteway, still out of breath. 'Who are you – boy?'

Geoffrey was brushing his trousers down, and Charlie and Sue and Jimmy joined us. Foxy lay quite still in my arms, delighted to be with me, quite unaware that he was the cause of all the trouble.

'How dare you – dare you jump on me like that!' went on Mr Whiteway. 'What are you doing here?'

'You were going to shoot the fox,' said Geoffrey. 'It's a tame fox, it's David's.'

'How – was I to know?' asked Mr Whiteway. 'They all look alike, don't they?'

'He's wearing a collar,' said Geoffrey.

'People shouldn't shoot foxes,' said Sue.

'Decent people don't,' said Charlie.

'Oh dear, I think I'm going to die,' moaned Mr Tidy.

'Nonsense,' said Mrs Whiteway. 'It's only a flesh wound. We'd better carry him down to the car.'

'Just a minute,' said Geoffrey. 'Let's take a few photographs.' And before anyone could stop him he was darting among us with his camera going click, click, click, taking photographs of Mr Whiteway examining his gun, Mr Tidy being helped up, one of the men still digging, and the tall goofy man collecting the sacks. The dogs were far away, sniffing at the aniseed trail.

'What are you up to?' asked Mr Whiteway. 'What's going on here?'

'Just taking some pictures,' said Geoffrey. 'Might come in useful.'

'Everything all right?' asked Jeremy, coming up behind. 'I blew the whistle directly I saw Foxy. He wouldn't stop for me, he was going full tilt.'

I stooped to put the fox on the lead.

'I thought I'd shut him in,' I said. 'He nearly upset everything.'

'Foxes shouldn't be allowed,' said Mr Whiteway, still examining his gun. 'They're vermin.'

'Nonsense,' said Sue. 'They don't do you any harm, any more than the badgers do. You just want to kill everything, that's your trouble.'

'So that's it – you wanted to protect the badgers, did you?'

'Why not?' asked Jeremy.

'They're not *your* badgers,' I said.

'I rent this ground,' said Mr Whiteway. 'It's virtually mine.'

'And all the living things on it and in the wood, I suppose,' said Geoffrey. 'And you make sure they don't live long.'

'Don't be impertinent, boy,' said Mr Whiteway. 'I didn't come here to argue with children.'

Sue said, 'Oh, you silly old buzzard, it's no good talking to you. All you know is how to fire your stupid old gun.'

'And shoot Mr Tidy,' said Jeremy.

'Rotten shot, you are,' said Charlie.

'Come on,' said Geoffrey, 'let's help Mr Tidy down to the road. No good wasting time talking to these apes.'

It took us over half an hour to move Mr Tidy down the hill, across the buttercup meadow to the station-wagon in the lane. Not that I did any carrying; the two men and the goofy fellow and Geoffrey managed all right, while Mr and Mrs Whiteway, Sue, Charlie, Jeremy, Jimmy, Clarence and I brought up the rear. But just as we came out of the wood, near the footpath stile, something very unfortunate happened.

'Look!' exclaimed Mr Whiteway suddenly, pointing skywards. The carrying party kept straight on, but Sue and I both stopped and I looked up. At first I couldn't see anything unusual, but apparently Mr Whiteway could, because in a second he had raised his gun towards the nearest tree and was taking aim, although I didn't know what at.

'Keep still, you brute!' he shouted, and then he fired the second barrel straight up at the tree and there was a fluttering and a loud squawk and down fell a small feathered object.

'Got him!' shouted Mr Whiteway. 'First shot! Bang on!' And he began to dance about with excitement.

'*Now* what have you done?' said Sue, and we both walked over to see what lay in the long grass. It took a minute to discover, but presently we found it, a small ball of feathers and blood, still warm, that only a few minutes earlier had been a young owl. I picked it up carefully, ashamed that anyone could shoot an owl sitting on a branch, a harmless, delightful-looking creature if ever there was one. I'd seen so many owls in our woods, and heard them calling at night, that I was quite shocked to see one unexpectedly and so suddenly killed in front of me.

I felt outraged, as if Mr Whiteway had killed something of my own, something I cared for. It was so needless, to kill the owl. I turned on him as he came up to me, and I was furious.

'What did you do *that* for?' I shouted. 'Why did you shoot that owl?'

He took the dead bird out of my hand and said, 'It's a Little Owl, a perishing nuisance to everyone, and we're well rid of it. It'll do nicely for my collection. I'll have it stuffed.'

'Someone ought to stuff *you*,' said Sue, just behind me.

'With stinging nettles,' added Jeremy.

'You didn't *have* to kill it,' I said. 'You didn't give it a chance.'

'The Little Owl is a pest,' said Mr Whiteway. 'A perishing nuisance to everyone. If you kids knew anything about farming you'd know *that*. Now, let's get on down to the car.' And he walked off to join his wife, dangling the poor little bird by its legs.

I thought to myself that one day the Whiteways would get what they deserved, if there was any justice in the world. How I hated him, walking ahead of me

with his shotgun under his arm, the enemy of everything I liked in our woods and fields, the spoiler of the
countryside.

'Yah!' shouted Charlie. 'Why don't you kill something your own size?'

'He couldn't,' said Jeremy. 'He'd never find anything fat enough.'

'Why don't you shut up?' said Clarence. 'It's only
an old owl, anyway.'

'But it looks better than you do even when it's
dead,' said Sue, giving him a push that sent him
straight into a patch of stinging nettles.

'Ow!' he shouted. 'You beastly girl!'

Sue laughed, and we ran to catch up the carrying
party, which was now halfway down the buttercup
meadow. We could see the station-wagon standing in
the lane but when we eventually reached it we were in
for a shock. For there, standing waiting for us, with
his bicycle propped against the hedge, was our new
village policeman, Mr Barrow. He is very tall and
thin and has a big, red moustache.

'Afternoon,' he said. 'What's all this 'ere then?'

'Good afternoon, Constable,' said Mrs Whiteway,
rather grandly.

Mr Tidy gave a moan of pain as they laid him on
the grass verge by the side of the road.

'What's wrong with 'im then?' asked Mr Barrow.

'There was an accident,' explained the tall goofy
man. 'Quite unintentional, you know. A gun went off

– pingo – right through the poor man's leg. But he's quite all right. Aren't you, Mr Tidy?'

'Oh – oh – oh!' murmured Mr Tidy.

'What's all that barking up there then?' demanded Mr Barrow, looking suspicious.

'Oh, that's nothing really,' said the goofy man.

'It's the dogs which were with us – they've got slightly out of control,' explained Mr Whiteway.

'What were you shooting up there?' Mr Barrow had produced a notebook and was writing in it.

'I wasn't actually shooting,' explained Mr Whiteway. 'We went into the wood to dig out some badgers.'

'Oh, badgers – eh? And what were *they* doing up there? Causing a disturbance?'

'They live up there, Constable,' said Mrs Whiteway. 'They live in holes in the ground.'

'I'm quite aware of that, madam. And you were spending your Sunday afternoon digging them out?'

'That's right,' said Mr Whiteway.

'Dangerous, are they?'

'No, not really.'

'And you were all out digging up badgers?'

'That's right, Constable, quite right. But we didn't actually find any – we didn't even see them. And now, if you don't mind, I'd like to go home. My wife and I will take Mr Tidy to the doctor. Not much damage done, I think.'

'He'll soon be up and about,' said Mrs Whiteway.

'Just a moment, sir,' said Mr Barrow. 'I haven't finished yet. This gun of yours – you hold a licence for it, I suppose?'

'My dear Constable, of course I do, quite up-to-date. In fact the wood over there is *mine*.'

'You own it, sir?'

'Not exactly, but I rent it. It's as good as mine.'

Mr Barrow looked Mr Whiteway up and down, and I don't think he quite liked what he saw. Whether the policeman was really anxious to catch him out, or whether he just felt Mr Whiteway was treating him in rather an off-hand manner, I never quite understood. But it seemed to me that Mr Barrow didn't think very much of Mr Whiteway, for he kept everyone standing there while he wrote down things in his notebook, and we all stood around in a group for quite a while, waiting.

At last the policeman looked up from his notes and said, 'And it was an accident, when you shot this gentleman in the leg?'

'Certainly. I've got plenty of witnesses.' Mr Whiteway glanced around, but we all looked blankly back at him, until the goofy man said:

'Of course it was an accident. He didn't *mean* to hit anyone. We all saw it happen.'

'I see,' said Mr Barrow, and made another note. 'And you only fired your gun once, and it hit the gentleman in the leg, by accident?'

Mr Whiteway looked indignant. 'That's what I said, Constable – once – and unfortunately Mr Tidy was hit. But nothing serious, you know.'

'He'll soon be as right as rain,' said Mrs Whiteway.

'With a stiff leg,' murmured Jeremy, just behind me.

Mr Barrow looked up from his notebook and eyed Mr Whiteway rather sharply.

'But I heard *two* gun shots,' he said. 'There was quite a long interval between them. I heard the first when I was down by the pond, and the second when I'd come up here.'

'Oh yes, Constable – there was another shot later, but that had nothing to do with it.'

'Nothing to do with *what*?'

'With Mr Tidy getting hit.'

The policeman wrote something more down in his notebook, and I felt rather glad it was old man Whiteway and not one of us who was being questioned. Mr Barrow was determined to be as difficult as possible.

'Look, sir,' he said, 'I don't think you're being quite straightforward with me. First of all you say there was only *one* shot, now you say there was two. Who else did you shoot?'

Mr Whiteway gave a little laugh, but it sounded rather weak. Then he said, 'No one, Constable. I'd quite forgotten about the second shot. It really isn't important. I shot a bird just as we were coming out of the wood,' and he held out his left hand, and there was the owl, all bloody.

'What's *that* then?' asked Mr Barrow.

'Only an owl – it's called the Little Owl, because it isn't quite so big as the Barn Owl or the Tawny Owl. No harm done, we're well rid of it.'

'Yes? Just a minute, sir.' Mr Barrow had started turning the pages of his notebook. 'Ah, here we are, sir. Owls. All owls, I see. Well, sir, it appears that you've broken the law.'

'Nonsense, my dear man,' said Mr Whiteway. 'There's no close season for owls. I haven't shot a partridge or a pheasant in June, and it isn't Christmas Day or Easter. So I'm perfectly within my rights. And killing badgers isn't illegal.'

'No,' said the policeman. 'Killing badgers isn't illegal, but killing owls is.'

'Owls? Surely not!'

'I'm afraid so, sir, owls are now protected by law.'

'But the Little Owl – that's a pest – a fearful nuisance – any farmer will tell you—'

Mr Barrow said, 'It's the gentlemen in Parliament that concern me, sir, not the farmers. They make the laws. Owls are now protected by law.'

'Since when?' asked Mr Whiteway.

'Since they brought in the new law,' said Mr Barrow.

'But that's ridiculous,' said Mrs Whiteway. 'It's only a tiny little—'

'Protected owl,' said Mr Barrow, 'which the gentleman has just shot.'

We all listened with growing admiration for our new policeman. It looked as if he had caught the Whiteways in exactly the way we wanted. But Mr Whiteway wasn't particularly upset.

'Well, Constable, let's talk about that later, shall we. Perhaps you'd like to look in for a drink this evening and we'll discuss the matter? Meanwhile, I think we should get Mr Tidy to the doctor.'

'Very well, sir. I'll be round to see you about seven.' And he closed his notebook. Then we all helped lift Mr Tidy into the back of the station-wagon, and as it drove away down the lane, and the goofy man and Clarence and the others started walking away, Mr Barrow wheeled his bicycle out from the hedge and prepared to mount.

'You kids had better nip off home,' he said. 'And no more badger-hunting.'

'We weren't after the badgers,' explained Geoffrey. 'We were trying to stop them from digging them out.'

'Oh,' said Mr Barrow, and for the first and last time that afternoon he allowed himself a slight smile, just at the corners of his mouth.

'I tell you what,' I said as we began to walk down the lane. 'Why don't you all come back and have tea with us at the farm? Mum won't mind.'

She did mind, at first, but once Geoffrey and Jeremy and Jimmy and young Whiting and Sue and Charlie and I were all seated around the big table in the parlour, eating fast, she thawed out a little and was really quite happy. She said afterwards that she'd never had so many people sitting down to eat all at once in the farmhouse. Luckily, she'd just baked some cakes. After tea, I saw our guests off at the top of the lane.

'I'll be going in the morning,' said Geoffrey. 'Nothing more to do here. I should really have been at my uncle's by now. Well, goodbye, David. And look after Foxy.'

Of course I would, all his life. And as the six of them set off down the lane I reflected that I would miss Geoffrey, who had been so helpful and got us all organized, and had probably saved the badgers' lives. He had certainly saved Foxy's.

' 'Bye!' he called as they came to the bend in the road. He waved his hand, and then they were out of sight. And as I turned and walked across the lawn to the farmhouse where Foxy was stretched out – full of cake – waiting for me in the porch, I heard the dogs still barking and running around among the aniseed up in the woods.

That's how our gang saved the badgers on that Sunday afternoon in June. Old Mr Tidy is up and about again, but he walks with a slight limp. Mr Barrow the policeman always gives me a little smile when he passes me on his bicycle. I haven't seen Geoffrey again, and I don't suppose I ever shall, but he sent me a postcard from Dorset, signed Geoffrey and Judy, with a photograph of an owl on the front. Charlie, Sue, Jeremy, Whiting, and Jimmy Norwell, they're all fine, and we're going swimming in the mill pond tomorrow. But I forgot to tell you about old Mr Whiteway. He made a terrible mistake. When Mr Barrow the policeman went to see him that evening, he tried to give him a pound note – to bribe him not to take any action. But instead Mr Barrow took him to court at Horsham and Mr Whiteway was fined ten shillings for shooting a protected bird, and twenty-five pounds for trying to bribe a policeman. What was worse, it was reported in all the newspapers.

It's quiet up our way these days because the White-ways don't go shooting any more. August has been sunny and we've spent most of our evenings down by the mill pond. The wheatfields along the Horsham road are now a deep golden brown; the trees in the orchard are heavy with plums of every colour; the honeysuckle around our front porch is in full flower. We went stacking hay all day yesterday, and we'll go again tomorrow. A few birds are still nesting – there is a family of reed-buntings down by the pond.

I've given up going to the cottage in the woods and the gang has been dissolved. Charlie says he's going to start a new secret society, with a membership entrance fee of half-a-crown, but I don't think I'll join. I'm saving up for our holiday at Brighton. We're going to take Foxy to a house where they let him sleep on my bed and we shall go on the piers, and swim at Black Rock.

I saw an owl yesterday quite close to the farm, and last week Foxy found a hedgehog on the lawn. He barked at it and it curled up in a prickly ball and he didn't dare go near. I haven't seen a badger again but I know they're still up in the wood because you can see the flies going in and out of the set. I expect they come out at night, snouting around in search of grubs. I don't think they'll be disturbed again, now the Whiteways are moving to London.

It's good to know we won the battle, and that the badgers weren't harmed. They've lived up there for years, and it's really their wood, isn't it? Foxy and I reckon so, anyway.

. . . . five, six, seven, eight – What do you appreciate?

Piccolo
COLOUR BOOKS

Great new titles for boys and girls from eight to twelve
Fascinating full-colour pictures on every page
Intriguing, authentic easy-to-read facts

DINOSAURS

SECRETS OF THE PAST

SCIENCE AND US

INSIDE THE EARTH

EXPLORING OTHER WORLDS

STORMS

SNAKES AND OTHER REPTILES

AIRBORNE ANIMALS

Piccolo
COLOUR BOOKS 25p EACH

Fit your pocket – Suit your purse

Where danger makes exciting history ...

Piccolo
TRUE ADVENTURES

A magnificent new series for boys and girls from eight to twelve

Full colour covers
Daring deeds
Vivid illustrations
Thrilling true stories

PIRATES AND BUCCANEERS

GREAT SEA MYSTERIES

HIGHWAYMEN AND OUTLAWS

HAUNTED HOUSES

GREAT AIR BATTLES

SUBMARINES

Piccolo
TRUE ADVENTURES 20p EACH

More gripping than any fiction

The best in fun – for everyone. . . .

Piccolo
GAMES AND PUZZLES

101 BEST CARD GAMES FOR CHILDREN
NUT-CRACKERS
Puzzles and Games to boggle the mind

FUN AND GAMES OUTDOORS
JUNIOR PUZZLE BOOKS
JUNIOR CROSSWORD BOOKS
The most popular children's crosswords in Britain

BRAIN BOOSTERS
CODES AND SECRET WRITING
Piccolo – Pick of the Puzzles 20p each

Piccolo
SUPERB STORIES – POPULAR AUTHORS

FOLLYFOOT
Monica Dickens. Based on the Yorkshire Television series

FOXY
John Montgomery

FOXY AND THE BADGERS
John Montgomery. David comes to Sussex from an orphanage and finds
an unusually appealing new friend . . .

THE JUNGLE BOOK
Rudyard Kipling

THE SECOND JUNGLE BOOK
Rudyard Kipling. The magic of Mowgli, child of the forest, whose
adventures made him every other child's hero

TALES FROM THE HOUSE BEHIND
by the author of the world-famous Diary of Anne Frank

20p EACH